BIGGLES OF THE INTERPOL

Biggles outwits the law-breakers of the
world – eleven separate stories.

Whether tidying up a case of cold-blooded
murder, stamping out a dope peddling organization,
or helping to put a stop to trouble
in West Africa Biggles comes
out on top every time.

D1421910

CAPTAIN W. E. JOHNS

BIGGLES
OF THE INTERPOL

KNIGHT BOOKS
the paperback division of Brockhampton Press

ISBN 0 340 04148 X

This edition first published 1968 by Knight Books,
the paperback division of Brockhampton Press Ltd, Leicester
Second impression 1970

Printed and bound in Great Britain by
Cox & Wyman Ltd, London, Reading and Fakenham

First published by Brockhampton Press Ltd 1965
Text copyright © 1966 Capt. W. E. Johns

CONTENTS

PUBLISHER'S NOTE

Readers will understand that since these stories were originally written, political situations throughout the world have changed very much, and are still changing. Scientific progress has made enormous advancement, and geographical boundaries have altered. But we feel that this will not affect in any way the enjoyment of the stories.

1

BIGGLES
WORKS OVERTIME

'DID you know a fellow named Eustace Bowden? He was for some time a club instructor at Gatwick.' Air Commodore Raymond, head of the Special Air Police, put the question to Air Detective-Inspector Bigglesworth, his chief operational pilot, as he entered his office at Scotland Yard.

'I've heard of him, and may have seen him about, but I can't say I knew him,' answered Biggles.

'Have you heard he's been killed in a crash on an attempt to break the solo light plane record to Cape Town?'

'I've heard that a burnt-out aircraft, with a body, presumably that of the pilot, in it has been found in the Sudan – if that's what you mean, sir.'

'The crash was found not very far from what we may suppose would be Bowden's line of flight. Who else could it be?'

Biggles shrugged. 'I've no idea. Why should a pilot of Bowden's experience be off course?'

'How would I know?'

'Did he make any signals?'

'No. Why should he? It was a fine night.'

'All the more reason why he should have been dead on his track.'

'Nobody else has been reported missing so it could only be Bowden.'

'I think probably you're right,' agreed Biggles, reaching for a cigarette. 'It certainly looks like that.'

The Air Commodore frowned. 'What do you mean by probably? Have you any doubts about it?'

'Not if the aircraft and the body have been identified.'

The Air Commodore became curt. 'You know as well as I do that in cases of fire it's almost impossible to identify a body. Bowden was burnt beyond any hope of recognition. Not only did the aircraft crash in flames but it set off a grass fire that made it impossible to get near it for some time.'

'Did anyone see the machine come down?'

'Apparently not. In fact, it was supposed that natives had started the fire as they often do, to burn off the dead grass and so to encourage the growth of new grass for grazing. Not until the fire had burnt itself out were the remains of an aircraft discovered by the District Officer sent out by the Resident Magistrate to investigate. As you can imagine, by that time there wasn't much left of the pilot; or the machine, beyond the metal parts. In any case it's unlikely that the machine would have been identified, as never before, to my knowledge, has one of that type been seen in Africa.'

Biggles nodded. 'There was something a little odd about that.'

'What do you mean – odd?'

'The machine was a new type, an Owlet, produced by the United States Aircom Corporation. It was a

four-seater developed for night work on feeder lines,
which means that speed was sacrificed for reliability
and slow landings. When I read of what Bowden intended to attempt I was a little puzzled. Not that it
was any business of mine.'

'Why were you puzzled?'

'Because, on the machine's official performance
figures, had Bowden flown on full throttle all the way
he could not have broken the record.'

'The engine might have been hotted up for the job.'

'Yes, I suppose that's possible. We could soon find
out. The British agent for the Owlet is Allan Hay, at
Gatwick. It was from there Bowden took off for the
flight. By the way, has his wife been informed?'

'I don't know. Why?'

'Because I should feel inclined to hold my hand until
it has been established definitely that the body found
is that of her husband.'

The Air Commodore's frown deepened. 'I see you're
in one of your difficult moods. What's at the bottom
of all this?'

Biggles smiled faintly. 'Where exactly was the
machine found?'

'North-east of Atbara.'

'That's east of the main route south.'

'Yes.'

'Then he must have been well off his course.'

'Maybe he was trying to keep clear of north-bound
traffic.'

'That, for a man out to break a record, would be
unusually considerate.' Biggles shook his head. 'No,
sir. If he was off course it was by accident. Who found
the crash?'

'An officer of the Resident Magistrate at the government post of Abu Kara. Does that satisfy you?'

Biggles shrugged his shoulders. 'I'm satisfied that he found an aircraft. I'm not questioning that, sir.'

The Air Commodore spoke with a sort of awful patience. 'Then what are you questioning? There was only one aircraft on that sector of the route that night and it was Bowden, who had refuelled at Heliopolis. It *must* have been Bowden.'

'You assume that it was Bowden. You don't *know*. Since I've been on this job one thing I've learned is that it isn't safe to assume anything.'

'Very well. I'll get the number of the engine of Bowden's machine from the makers and have it checked with the one in the wreck. The engine, if nothing else, will have survived the fire. Will that satisfy you?'

'Not entirely.'

'In heaven's name, man! What more do you want?'

'Even if the check proved correct, and the number tallied, it would still do no more than confirm it was Bowden's machine. It wouldn't answer for the body. How could it?'

The Air Commodore sat back. 'You know, Bigglesworth,' he said slowly and deliberately, 'there are times when this relentless passion of yours over meticulous detail tries my patience. Everyone except you has accepted Bowden's death without question.'

'That's because it's the easiest course to take. Some people will do anything to avoid a spot of trouble.'

'There's no way of identifying a body charred to a cinder. Why not let it go at that?'

'Maybe there's something in my system that jibs at

taking for granted what everyone else takes for granted.' Biggles smiled. 'After all, sir, you have only yourself to blame for that. It was you, many years ago, when I was a junior flying officer, who hammered home in me the importance of little things.'

The Air Commodore sighed, nodding slowly. 'There you go. Up to your old trick of sliding the onus of responsibility on me. Very well. Have it your way. What do you suggest we do about it?'

Biggles spoke seriously. 'As this is a matter of life or death I think we should settle beyond all doubt that the body is that of Bowden before we say so. More than one man, presumed dead, has reappeared to upset quite a number of apple-carts. If you say Bowden's dead, and later on he were to turn up, we would all look pretty silly. For the moment, at any rate, you need merely say that Bowden is missing.'

'Delaying tactics.'

'Call it that if you like, but it gives us time.'

'All right. Time for what? How are you going to settle the question?'

'It shouldn't be difficult. Bowden served for some years in the R.A.F. In his medical papers there will be a dental chart. Get a copy of it and compare it with the teeth of the body found in the aircraft. That's been done before. Few sets of teeth are identical so there's your answer. Send a radio signal asking the Resident Magistrate to postpone interment pending identification and I'll fly out with Bowden's dental chart. At the same time you might ask him to get the District Medical Officer to make a pattern of the teeth they have there for comparison. I don't want to fiddle about with a corpse.'

'You're making this a grim business.'

'Inquests always are grim, but they're necessary. It's a million to one that the body is that of Bowden, and I shall be as surprised as you if it isn't; but we shall at least have proved the point. You might get particulars of Bowden's career. I'll have a look at the crash. I don't suppose it'll be possible to ascertain the cause – you know how it is – but no harm will be done by looking. We shall then have done everything possible. I'll have a word with Hay, at Gatwick, before I leave. The makers of the machine will be puzzled, no doubt, and perhaps upset. It's no advertisement for them.'

'All right. Let's leave it at that for the time being,' agreed the Air Commodore. 'You go to Gatwick and have a word with Hay about this if you like, but I can't imagine how he'll be able to help you.'

'Okay, sir. You get that dental chart for me, and no matter what Hay says about it I'll slip out to Africa and check up.'

Biggles returned to Air Police Headquarters to tell Ginger what was in the wind, Algy and Bertie being on leave.

Two days later, Biggles, who had flown to the Sudan with Ginger in a police Proctor, was shown by a coloured sentry into the headquarters of the Resident Magistrate at the government post of Abu Kara. Even as he introduced himself to the two men present, one of whom turned out to be the District Medical Officer, he sensed an 'atmosphere'.

'You have had a signal from my chief, I believe, so you would be expecting me,' he began, looking from one to the other.

'Yes, and we're glad you've come,' answered the magistrate. 'Something queer, not to say unpleasant, has turned up.'

'Indeed?'

'Yes. It enables me to tell you why the machine crashed.'

Biggles stared. 'You can tell me why it crashed?'

'Yes. The pilot was shot.'

'*Shot!*' Biggles looked incredulous. 'You – er – mean he was hit by a random bullet from the ground?'

The doctor spoke. 'Not at all. The bullet that killed him couldn't possibly have come from the ground. It was fired in the air, and moreover, at close range. Death must have been instantaneous.'

Biggles was still staring. 'Forgive me, sir, if I seem sceptical, but how could you judge the range, considering the whole thing was burnt out?'

'From the hole in the skull and the type of weapon used.' The doctor pointed to a small object on the desk. 'There's the bullet. A lead bullet, fired, so the station armourer assures me, from a Webley forty-five revolver. I should never have found it had you not asked for a description of the pilot's dental formation, for as you will believe, I wasn't looking for anything like *that*. The bullet entered the head from the side just below the temple, struck the opposite cheek-bone and lodged in the jaw. Which means that it travelled *downwards*; and that in turn can only mean that the shot was fired in the air. Had it come from the ground, or at any rate below the machine, it must have travelled upwards.'

'Excuse me, gentlemen. Do you mind if I sit down?' said Biggles.

Not for a long time had Ginger seen him so shaken.

'This is a development for which I was not prepared,' went on Biggles, taking a sheet of paper, actually a Service form, from his pocket, and handing it to the Medical Officer. 'That is the dental chart of the man who was officially flying the aircraft,' he stated. 'How does it compare with the one you have?'

The doctor did little more than glance at the chart. 'These teeth are not those of the body we found in the crash. The teeth of the body we have here are perfect and complete. This chart you have given me shows that five molars are missing. It is the mouth, I would say, of an older man.'

Again for a moment Biggles could only stare. The truth of the matter was, in spite of the arguments he had put forward to the Air Commodore, he was convinced in his mind that the crash could only be that of Bowden, the ill-fated record-breaker. He looked at Ginger. 'If it wasn't Bowden's machine, who on earth could it have been? No one else is missing. If it wasn't Bowden in the crash it couldn't have been his machine. Or could it? This has me stumped.' Biggles shook his head.

The magistrate resumed. 'In the matter of the machine, if it's any help to you I can tell you the number of the engine. I sent a man out to get it.'

'What is it?'

'J.B. 4257.'

'J.B. 4257,' repeated Biggles, in a dazed voice. 'Then it *must* have been Bowden's machine, for that's the number of his engine. I got it from the agent before I left.' Again he looked at Ginger. 'We seem to have

started something, and given ourselves a pretty tangle
to unravel. It was the machine in which Bowden left
England but he wasn't flying it when it crashed. Who
was flying it? The plane crashed because the pilot was
shot. Who fired the shot. As only one body was found
in the crash quite obviously Bowden couldn't have
been in it. Where is he?'

'According to Hay,' reminded Ginger, 'Bowden
wore a parachute. You remember Hay telling us that.
He told Hay, who was surprised to see him carrying
one on such a trip, that having to wear one for so long
in the R.A.F. he felt uncomfortable in the air without
one.'

'The man who died in the aircraft had no parachute,
I can assure you of that,' put in the magistrate. 'Had
that been so we should have found the metal fittings.
Wondering why the man hadn't jumped if he was in
trouble I looked particularly for them. That, of course,
was before the doctor found the bullet.'

'As he was shot through the head a brolly wouldn't
have been much use to him, anyway,' muttered Biggles
grimly. He drew a deep breath. 'After all this there
doesn't seem much point in our looking at the wreck-
age. May I ask you, gentlemen, to keep the soft pedal
on this until I've had a chance to confer with my
chief? I'll go straight back. Obviously there has been
foul play here and it looks uncommonly like a deliberately planned murder.'

'Do you want to see the body? We held up interment as requested.'

'No thanks. You've told me all I need to know about
it.'

'Then we may bury it.'

'Certainly. I assume you found nothing in the pockets that would help identification?'

'Not a thing. Everything was incinerated.'

'I see. The problem now is to find Bowden. It seems futile to look for him in a country this size but should you hear of him, dead or alive, you'd oblige me by sending a signal at once to Scotland Yard.'

The magistrate promised to do that.

'That's all, then,' said Biggles. 'Thanks for your co-operation, sir. We'll press on home.'

In a few minutes the Proctor was speeding northwards.

'Now you *have* let yourself in for something,' remarked Ginger.

'I'm beginning to think I should have taken the Air Commodore's advice and left well alone,' answered Biggles lugubriously.

When Biggles reached the Yard and walked into his chief's office he was greeted with a smile.

'You're soon back,' observed the Air Commodore. 'I assume you must have now satisfied yourself that it was Bowden?'

'Far from it,' answered Biggles wearily, sinking into a chair. 'It was Bowden's machine all right but he wasn't in it.'

The Air Commodore's expression changed abruptly. 'Not in it? Who was?'

'I haven't a clue – and in this case there's no dental chart for comparison.'

'All right. Don't rub it in.' The Air Commodore pushed over the cigarette box. 'You know, Bigglesworth, you must have an instinct for this sort of thing.'

'If that's so it's my misfortune, for it gives me an awful lot of trouble.'

'I withdraw my criticism of your methods. Now tell me about it.'

Biggles recounted the result of his investigations at Abu Kara. 'I seem to have set myself a pretty problem,' he concluded. 'What on earth can have happened to Bowden? You say no news has been received from Africa, so it's a case of where do we go from here.'

'You tell me,' requested the Air Commodore, helplessly.

'For a start I think I'll run down to Gatwick and have another word with Hay,' decided Biggles. 'He has an interest in this and may be able to throw light on the business. While I'm away you might get Bowden's full service record from the Ministry. To know where he's been and what he's done might help. It's queer he hasn't shown up. He's either dead or deliberately keeping under cover. If he was wearing a brolly, as Hay said, he should still be alive.'

'It must have been one or the other,' agreed the Air Commodore. 'It does seem queer that he hasn't turned up.'

'I shan't be long,' said Biggles, and taking Ginger with him went by car to Gatwick where they found Hay, the Aircom agent, at his desk.

'Hello! What's your trouble?' greeted Hay, for he knew Biggles fairly well, and of his connection with the Air Police.

'I'm still working on this accident to one of your machines in Africa,' informed Biggles, accepting a cigarette.

'I've already told you all I know about it,' declared Hay. 'The aircraft was in perfect order when it left here. I can't imagine what happened. Your guess is as good as mine. My people are pretty sick about it. What was intended to be a publicity stunt has ended up in a mess that will do us more harm than good. I'm partly to blame.'

'How so?'

'I should never have agreed to the show. I had a feeling that Bowden was phoney.'

Biggles frowned. 'What gave you that idea?'

'Well, for one thing he hadn't any money.'

'He had enough to buy the machine.'

'He didn't pay for it.'

'Why didn't you tell me this before?'

'The less said about a bad show like this the better.'

'Who did pay for the machine? I imagine you didn't give it to him.'

'A lad named Renford – Antony Renford.'

'How does he come into the picture?'

'He was a pupil pilot at the club here. Bags of money. That's how he got to know Bowden. Bowden was an instructor here at one time. He must have put up the proposition to young Renford, who fell for it. At all events he bought the machine.'

'Why buy a machine? Was he going on the flight?'

'Not so far as I know. The trip was supposed to be a solo job. Nice lad, Renford. He's only about nineteen. This business must have cost him a packet.'

'Why should he buy a machine for someone else to fly?'

'Search me.'

'Can you give me his address?'

'Sure. Here it is. He lived alone in a flat in Jermyn Street.'

Biggles picked up the slip of paper, folded it and put it in his pocket. 'I take it Bowden chose the machine, not Renford?'

'Correct.'

'Do you know why Bowden chose an Owlet?'

Hay grinned. 'Because it's a good aeroplane.'

'Didn't it strike you as odd that he, a practical pilot, should pick on a plane which couldn't do what he said he intended to do?'

'This isn't a pilot's information bureau. My job is to sell aeroplanes to anybody who wants one, without asking why he wants it. Bowden had the money to pay, I had the machine to sell.'

'You're sure there was nothing special about the airframe or engine?'

'It was a standard model. I told you that the other day.'

'I just wanted to be quite sure. A lot might depend on it. Well, if that's as much as you can tell me I'll push along.'

'That's all I know. The thing's as much a mystery to me as it is to you. I want to forget it. It won't help me to sell Owlets.'

'And now,' said Ginger, when they were outside, 'I suppose we're on our way to see this lad Renford.'

'We are. But I have a feeling he won't be at home.'

'Why not?'

'Because if I'm any good at guessing he's dead and buried – in Africa. If he put up the money for that machine you may be sure he expected to do the trip with Bowden – no matter what Bowden told the Press about flying solo. The more I think about it the more sure I am that Bowden never intended to try to break the Cape record. As an experienced pilot he would know that the machine was incapable of it. That doesn't make sense. What was his object? I'm afraid Renford insisted on going, which may not have suited Bowden, and as a result the boy lost his life. At least, that's how it begins to look to me. There are still a lot of questions to be answered, though. The first is, why did Bowden acquire an aircraft only to destroy it? It sounds daft, but I'm pretty sure that's what he did. But when we know the answer to that we shall know the rest.'

'You think Bowden is still alive?'

'I do. He took a parachute. Why? Because he felt more comfortable in it? Rot. He took that brolly for a more practical purpose than that.'

Biggles' surmise about the man they had called to see was confirmed at the entrance to the block of flats. A uniformed janitor was on duty.

'I've called to see Mr Renford,' announced Biggles.

'I'm sorry, sir, but Mr Renford is not at home.'

'Do you know when he'll be back?'

'No, sir. He didn't say.'

'When did you last see him?'

The janitor pursed his lips. 'Let's see. Must be ten days ago.'

'He didn't say where he was going, or what he was going to do?'

'No, sir.'

'And you've heard nothing of him since he went away?'

'No, sir.'

'Thank you.'

Biggles returned to the car and drove on towards Scotland Yard.

'If Bowden murdered young Renford he'll be clear away by now,' observed Ginger, moodily.

'That may be so; but if he assumes that he has been reported dead he may take a chance and give himself away,' returned Biggles. 'That must have been all very carefully planned, although for what purpose I wouldn't try to guess. No doubt Bowden's imagining by now that he's got away with it. We shall see.'

They went on to the Air Commodore's office and reported the latest developments.

'Did you find anything of interest in Bowden's service papers?' inquired Biggles.

'No. His career was fairly normal, except that he was in a spot of trouble once or twice, on one occasion being under suspicion of having misappropriated squadron funds. But nothing was proved. He lived apart from his wife. His longest overseas tour was at Suakin, on the Red Sea, with a flying-boat squadron. That was some time ago. The station has since been abandoned.'

Biggles' eyebrows went up. 'That's no great distance from where the Owlet crashed. Could that be a co-incidence? At all events, he would know the country round Suakin very well.'

'And on the other side of the Red Sea too, apparently. He once had a forced landing on the Arabian coast just south of Jidda, and spent a couple of pleasant weeks, waiting for a relief plane, with a friend of ours named Sheikh Ibn Usfa. Later, he fetched him to be the guest of honour at a squadron guest night.'

'I see,' said Biggles slowly. 'Why did he leave the Service?'

'He resigned. I've found out that he was hopelessly in debt, so as he couldn't meet his bills it's likely he would have been asked to resign, anyway.'

'I wonder,' breathed Biggles.

'What do you wonder?'

'If he's resumed his friendship with the Sheikh? He must have found a snug hiding-place somewhere or we should have heard something of him by this time – dead or alive.'

'How could he have crossed the Red Sea without an aircraft? The Owlet was burnt out. There's no longer any doubt about that.'

'There are such things as boats, and having been stationed at Suakin he'd know his way around,' averred Biggles. 'As a clue it is, I must admit, pretty thin; but I can think of nowhere else to look. There may be some hook-up. If he isn't there he might be anywhere between Cairo and the Cape.'

'Very well,' said the Air Commodore. 'You started this so it's up to you to find him. You might run out to Suakin and see if there's any news there. Failing in that go over and have a word with the Sheikh. He might be able to help you, or maybe drop something that would give you a line on Bowden's whereabouts. They seem to have got quite pally.'

'It's better than doing nothing,' agreed Biggles. 'We can't keep the lid on this business much longer or when the facts *are* released the newspapers will want to know why the secrecy.'

'You might care to see this,' said the Air Commodore, taking a photograph from the file and passing it across the desk. 'It was taken on the occasion of the Sheikh's visit to the squadron at Suakin. There he is, in the middle, with the Commanding Officer on his right and Bowden on his left. The rest are officers who were serving with the unit at the time.'

Biggles studied the photograph, and Ginger, looking over his shoulder, did the same. The Sheikh, unmistakable in his Arab dress, was a fine, aristocratic-looking man of about seventy. Bowden was a heavy, rather florid type, with the big moustache in vogue in the R.A.F.

Biggles handed it back. 'Thanks,' he said. 'I shall know Bowden if I see him. If that's all, sir, we'll move off.'

It was five days before Biggles with Ginger took up a course across the Red Sea, having stopped at Alexandria to make some inquiries, and later at Abu Kara, where he renewed his acquaintance with the Resident Magistrate. There was no further news. Bowden, it seemed, had vanished as utterly as a stone dropped in deep water. With a letter of introduction in his pocket Biggles then pushed on for his final objective, the oasis and village of El Bishra where the Sheikh had his palace.

There was no difficulty in finding it on a coast so barren that settlements are few and far between. There was no airfield. In fact there was really no need for one, for the *sabkha*, flat areas of sand and pebbles, stretched for miles in every direction except to the west, where forbidding cliffs held back the sea. Biggles

landed as near as he dare to the village. There was no
one about, so having switched off they began walking
towards the palace, a whitened mud-brick building
that stood high above the huddle of sun-bleached
houses. The only green things were the usual date
palms that thrust their crowns high into the steely-blue
sky, and even their fronds hung motionless, wilting in
the blistering heat.

A man appeared. He saw them and instantly retired.
More came out, and it seemed to Ginger that there
was something hostile about the way they just stood
there watching the approach of the two white men.

'I don't know that I quite like this,' he remarked.

'A few years ago they would probably have knocked
our heads off,' returned Biggles lightly. 'But times
have changed. In any case, according to the Air Commodore we've always been on good terms with this
particular Sheikh, who was educated in England. It's
no more than curiosity. They can't have many visitors
here.'

Ginger was glad of the reassurance, for there was
something disconcerting, to say the least of it, in the
way the Arabs with dark scowling faces, but without
saying a word, lined up beside them and kept them
company. By the time they reached the palace they
were in the centre of a small but menacing crowd.

'Something's happened here or they wouldn't be-
have like this,' asserted Biggles quietly. 'I hope
nothing's happened to the Sheikh. That would make
things awkward.'

At the palace door they were stopped by two armed
Negroes, but Biggles was saved the trouble of explaining his reason for being there when a young man, from

his dress a person of importance, appeared from within.

'Can I be of service to you?' he inquired, in perfect English.

'May I have the honour of an audience with the Sheikh Ibn Usfa?' requested Biggles.

The young man appeared to hesitate for a moment. Then he said, with a frank, disarming smile: 'Please come in. My house and all that is in it is at your disposal.'

They followed their host into a spacious room, simply furnished. 'Please be seated,' he said, indicating a divan. 'You would like some refreshment after your journey – some sherbet, or some coffee perhaps?'

'Thank you. Some sherbet would be welcome. It's rather warm outside.'

The sheikh clapped his hands. A Negro appeared, accepted an order in what presumably was Arabic, bowed and retired.

'May I, if I may speak without offence, congratulate you on your command of my language?' said Biggles.

A smile, rather sad, softened the young man's face. 'It will not seem so remarkable when I tell you that I have just completed my third year at your Cambridge University. I returned only a few days ago, on receiving news of my father's death.'

Biggles' expression changed. 'Your father . . .?'

'The Sheikh Ibn Usfa was my father. He is dead. Such was God's will.'

Biggles began to get up. 'I am most dreadfully sorry,' he said quickly. 'I didn't know. We will not intrude on –'

The young sheikh raised a hand. 'There's no need to apologize. Please remain. I would like to tell you about this tragic affair. You may be able to throw some light on the matter. You see, my father, who never harmed any man, was murdered.'

'*Murdered!* By whom?' Biggles was aghast.

'We don't know. All we know is that a man who must have been familiar with this house came here in the dead of night. He killed the sentry on duty, entered this room, shot my father and fled.'

Biggles' face was pale in spite of the heat. 'When did this happen?'

'A fortnight ago. When I received the news I flew straight home, of course.'

'And you have no idea who did this foul thing?'

'No. But I know *why* he did it. My father, like many sheikhs along this coast, was a great collector of pearls, as was his father before him. Fine pearls are found in these waters as you probably know, and our men dive for them. My father's collection stood on this table, in sea water, in ordinary glass jars, so that he could always see them. You may think it foolish that a fortune in pearls should be left thus, but to my father, who was an honest man, it was inconceivable that anyone would touch them. They have stood here for years. Well, they have gone. It was for them, obviously, that the murderer came. But let me not burden you with my troubles. Can I serve in place of my father, whom you wished to see?'

'It is possible,' said Biggles slowly, after exchanging glances with Ginger, 'that my business here is not unconnected with what you have just told me. We are police officers from London. Did anyone, here or in the village, hear an aircraft on the night your father was murdered?'

'Yes. As a matter of fact an aeroplane was heard; but as that is not unusual it was not connected with my father's death.'

'Did anyone hear this aircraft land?'

'No.'

'How was the sentry killed?'

'By a blow on the head with a heavy weapon.'

'Such as the butt end of a revolver?'

'Yes, I suppose that might have done it, as would any blunt instrument.'

'But I don't understand. How could that happen? I mean, if the sentry saw a stranger surely he would challenge him before the intruder was close enough to strike him.'

'One would think so.'

'But if the visitor was a man whom he thought he recognized as a friend of your father's he would not raise an alarm.'

'Of course not. He would welcome him with a greeting.'

'Had that happened it would account for the sentry being caught off guard.'

'That could be the explanation. Indeed, it would be difficult to think of another. The sentry would certainly bar the approach of a stranger, black or white.'

'I will not weary you with the details of another murder on the opposite coast into which I am inquiring,' went on Biggles. 'But as it is possible that both murders were committed by the same man I must ask you, if you will, to bear with me a little longer. It is now in your interest as well as mine.'

'I am entirely at your disposal.'

At this juncture refreshments were brought in and there was a pause in the proceedings.

'Did you ever meet a man here, a Royal Air Force officer, named Bowden?' resumed Biggles.

'I never met him but I heard of him from my father.'

'He was a guest here for some time, about three years ago.'

'So I understand. I had just left for Cambridge.'

'Would the sentry know this man Bowden?'

'Almost surely, for he had grown old in my father's service.'

'In which case he would not challenge him?'

'No. He would receive him with respect.'

'I imagine Bowden would see the pearls when he was here?'

'He could hardly fail to do so. They stood on the table and were never locked up. Anyway, my father would be proud to show them to him, for they were his hobby. Every one was a specimen. Smaller or misshapen ones he sold to a dealer.'

'Who was this dealer?'

'A Greek named Janapoulos, of Suakin, on the opposite coast.'

'Would you recognize these pearls if you saw them again?'

'The exceptional ones, perhaps. My father knew them like his children. No two pearls are exactly alike. Apart from size, colour, weight and lustre, there are always minute marks, sometimes tiny cracks, observable only through a magnifying glass, which make every large pearl an individual. My father kept a little book in which was noted a description of every pearl in his collection. As I have said, it was his hobby. There is little else for a man to do here.'

'Would it be too much to ask you to lend me that book?'

'You may have it if it will help to bring my father's murderer to justice.' The young sheikh smiled sadly. 'It is not much use without the pearls.'

'Without it, it would not be possible to identify the pearls, which are certain to turn up somewhere, sooner or later. About this Greek at Suakin. Did your father go to him when he had pearls to sell, or did the man come here?'

'He called here at intervals to see if my father had anything to offer. He called on other sheikhs too, of course. He has a boat which takes him on his tours up and down the coast.'

'Would you regard him as an honest man?'

'He has that reputation, and my father must have found him so, or he would have had nothing to do with him.'

'Are there any other pearl dealers near here?'

'Only small men. Janapoulos is the best known. He is known in London and Paris, I believe.'

'Has he a shop in Suakin?'

'No. He lives in a private house, the Villa Verde, in the Stretta Gonzales.' The Sheikh frowned. 'You don't think he –?'

'Stole the pearls? Not for a moment. As a professional dealer he would know they might be recognized when they were put up for sale. He would hardly be such a fool as to risk his reputation. But he may be able to help us.'

'In what way?'

'The thief may have offered the pearls to him.'

'Even so I don't think he would recognize them because my father allowed no one but himself to actually handle them. Moreover, those pearls are the last thing Janapoulos would expect to see in Suakin. He would know as well as anyone that they were never allowed to leave this house.'

'Still, he may have heard rumours.' Biggles got up. 'Do not think us discourteous if we leave at once, but as you will appreciate, time is now of vital importance.'

'I understand. If I can be of further assistance do not hesitate to call on me.'

'Thank you.'

Biggles and Ginger took their leave and returned to the aircraft.

'A nice chap, that,' remarked Ginger, as Biggles, finding a spot of shade under a wing, paused to light a cigarette.

'The thief who murdered his father might have turned a friend of ours into an enemy – particularly as it begins to look as if it may have been a Britisher. But a crook never thinks of that.'

'You think Bowden did it?'

'I hate to think so, but all the evidence so far points to that and we can't get away from it. Let's sum it up. Bowden was broke. He knew the pearls were there, unguarded except for a sentry who knew him as a friend of the Sheikh. He knew his way about the palace. An aircraft was heard that night. He had one. At least, he had one until he crashed it in Africa. The reason he had one is wide open to suspicion. Ostensibly it was for a go at the Cape record. That, on the face of it, was ridiculous. He must have known the machine

chosen was incapable of it. Why did he choose an
Owlet, designed for night work, when, as he wasn't
paying for it he could presumably have had a faster
machine? No doubt he could have had any machine he
chose to name. The Owlet has been found burnt out,
but the body in it wasn't his. How did that happen?
Where is he? If he wasn't after the pearls what was he
after? He was certainly after something, and if it was
on the level why hasn't he shown up?'

'It looks pretty black,' agreed Ginger. 'And don't
forget Bowden's service record wasn't too good.'

'Let's glance at it from another angle,' went on
Biggles. 'The only way a white man could get here,
without making a long, difficult and dangerous journey, would be by air. Bowden was a pilot. All he
needed was an aircraft. He knew young Renford. He
knew he was mad on flying and had plenty of money.
The suggestion of a record flight would find him a
ready listener. Renford, too, has disappeared, and a
reasonable assumption would be that it was his body
found in the plane – for which, don't forget, he paid.'

'Could Renford have been party to the robbery?'

'I'd say not. He was more concerned with flying than
with pearls. He had plenty of money, anyway. All
Bowden had to do was land on the *sabkha*, as we did,
and leaving Renford to take care of the machine, walk
on to the palace, get the pearls and make his get-away.
I may be on the wrong track, but these factors all fit
so well that we're forced to these conclusions. If I'm
right it was a devilish scheme, for he must have deter-
mined all along to kill Renford.'

'Why did Bowden have to kill him?'

'That's pretty obvious. What actually happened in

the plane we may never know. Renford, wondering what Bowden was doing, may have asked awkward questions. It's my belief that from the outset part of Bowden's plan was to kill him because that would serve two vital purposes. Not only would it dispose of a possible danger but it would appear as if he, Bowden, was dead. There would be no fuss, no bother. In a day or two the crash would be forgotten. All very simple. Why, we may ask, did Bowden clutter himself up with a parachute? Was he nervous? Not likely. It was all part of the plan. Renford had no brolly or the buckle, or the ring, would have been found in the crash. All Bowden had to do was shoot his partner and step out. No one would suspect murder, and no one would connect a jewel robbery in Arabia with an accident in Africa. Why should they? It was clever — devilish clever. It's true I argued the question of identification with the chief, but in my mind I was sure that the body in the crash was that of Bowden. Which shows how easy it is to be wrong.'

'You suspected something phoney?'

'Not exactly phoney, and certainly not murder. I was curious about the alleged purpose of the flight in a machine that would have to perform a miracle to succeed. For the rest, one thing has led to another. We'll now call on this Greek pearl dealer in Suakin. If Bowden knew him, as is not unlikely, as he once served here, he may have gone to him to sell some pearls for ready money, which he would need.'

'That's a wide shot.'

'Not so wide as you think. If you look at the map you'll see that the crash occurred not far from one of the few railways in that area, the line that runs from

Atbara to Suakin and Port Sudan. That may have been
a fluke, but as Bowden's plan, as we see it, was so well
thought out, I suspect it was not. He wouldn't want to
walk far across that sort of country.'

'You believe that having shot Renford he jumped,
leaving the machine to crash?'

'I do.'

'He then made his way to the railway and boarded
a train?'

'Yes.'

'For Suakin?'

'Yes, either because he knew a pearl dealer there or
because he could board a boat to get him out of the
country. We shall see. That's enough talking. Let's get
cracking.'

The short run to the African coast was soon made,
and within two hours they were in the narrow street in
the ancient port of Suakin wherein dwelt the man who
bought the Sheikh's surplus pearls. Finding the villa
after a little trouble they were informed that he was at
home, and were presently received by him in his office.

'I understand, Mr Janapoulos, that you sometimes
have pearls for sale?' began Biggles.

The Greek conceded that this was so. His manner
was smooth and courteous.

'We are interested only in the very highest quality.'

Janapoulos made a gesture of regret. 'I am sorry,'
he said sadly. 'I am a poor man and cannot afford to
deal in pearls of such value. A pity. Had you given me
warning of your coming, or had you been here a few
days ago, we might have made a transaction.'

'You mean, you had some?' prompted Biggles.

B

'Some were brought to me. They were very fine. Too fine, much too magnificent, alas, for my small purse.'

'May I ask who brought these pearls to you?'

There Biggles may have been a little too abrupt, for the Greek's eyes narrowed with suspicion. 'I make it a rule never to discuss my clients,' he said curtly. 'You will appreciate that.'

Biggles conceded the point and went on another tack. 'We are friends of the Sheikh Ibn Usfa. I believe you knew him.'

'Indeed. I know him well. A noble gentleman, and a very good customer of mine.'

Biggles spoke slowly, with his eyes on the man's face. 'Did you know that he has been murdered?'

There was nothing false about the Greek's consternation. His dark eyes filled with horror and the colour fled from his cheeks. 'Murdered,' he gasped. 'Is it possible? How? By whom?'

'That is what I am trying to discover,' replied Biggles quietly. 'In the hope that you will be frank with me I will be frank with you. We are detectives from London. We have just come from El Bishra, where we were told by the Sheikh's son of your dealings with the Sheikh Usfa. It was thought you might help us.'

'But how? What could I know?'

'The Sheikh's collection of pearls was stolen by the murderer. Now you will understand my purpose in coming to you.'

The Greek's agitation was almost painful to watch. For a moment he was unable to speak. Then he blurted: 'But you don't think that I –'

'No – no,' Biggles consoled him. 'But you must

understand that everyone in the district will be under suspicion until we arrive at the truth. I have been assured that your reputation is of the highest.'

'I will tell you all I know, although that isn't much,' said the pearl dealer, moistening his lips. 'Had you told me at the beginning –'

'Never mind that,' interposed Biggles. 'Who brought these fine pearls to you? Was it a white man – an Englishman?'

'Yes.'

'Had you ever seen him before?'

'Yes, but it was some years ago. I had forgotten him. He was an officer of the Royal Air Force, stationed here.'

'Can you recall his name?'

The Greek searched his memory. 'It escapes me. Rew . . . Bow . . .'

'Bowden?'

'That is the name.'

'How did you come to meet him?'

'I saw him twice. The first time was at El Bishra, at the palace, where he was a guest of the Sheikh Usfa. We spoke of pearls. Later, he came to me here. He said one day, when he was finished with flying, if he bought a boat for pearl fishing would I buy his pearls.'

'And you said yes?'

'Of course. Pearls are my business.'

'Yet when he came the other day, bringing some pearls, you did not buy them. Why?'

'I have told you the reason. I could not afford such specimens.'

'Was that the only reason?'

'No. To be truthful I was a little suspicious when he would not tell me how he came to have them. One must be careful.'

'In other words you suspected the pearls had been stolen?'

'Frankly, I thought that might have been so. I wasn't sure. I had no proof. I was puzzled because I hadn't heard of any pearls being stolen, and here news travels fast.'

'I can believe that,' murmured Biggles. 'So you bought none.'

'I bought one, a small one, because this man Bowden was in urgent need of money. I have it here – in my safe.'

'You didn't recognize it as part of the Sheikh's collection?'

'No. As God is my judge. Why should I? I did not know the Sheikh Usfa's pearls intimately. I have never handled them. Besides, knowing that he would never part with his pearls was another reason why the thought did not occur to me that they might be his. Please, how could I imagine that a white gentleman would do such a thing as this?' The Greek looked really distressed.

'Where else could such pearls have come from?' questioned Biggles, eyeing the man suspiciously.

The Greek threw out his hands. 'My dear sir, almost every sheikh along the Arabian coast collects pearls. This has been going on for centuries. Sometimes a dishonest diver will keep one, but he is soon found out. I did not trust this man Bowden; looking back I don't think I ever did trust him entirely, and thinking he may have acquired the pearls by some illegal method I

decided to put one in my safe in case inquiries should
be made.'

'How much did you pay for it?'

'About five hundred pounds.'

'About? Don't you know exactly?'

'No. It would depend on the current rate of ex-
change. The money was paid, at his request, partly in
Egyptian pounds, partly in dollars, but mostly in
French francs.'

'You mean you paid him in cash – in notes.'

'Yes. He asked for the money that way.'

'That in itself must have made you suspicious.'

The Greek shrugged. 'Perhaps.'

'Did he say why he wanted francs?'

'No, but I thought I knew. A French boat, the
Charbonniere, was due to call, bound for Marseilles.'

'Did he take it?'

'Yes.'

'How do you know that?'

'I watched him.'

'Why were you so interested in his movements?'

'I wanted to know where the pearls were going. It
could have been to my advantage. Bowden asked me
where he could best dispose of his pearls and I said of
course in Paris. It is the great pearl market of the
world. I gave him the name and address of the firm
there, Cortons, in the Rue de la Paix, to whom I send
customers with pearls too expensive for the local
markets. In fact, I gave him a note of introduction. I
could do that because Cortons know me quite well.'

'And you get a rake-off on such sales?'

'Certainly. Why not?'

'No reason at all, Mr Janapoulos.' Biggles picked up

his hat. 'Thank you very much for your assistance. You have been most helpful and I shall bear it in mind.'

'This will not mean trouble for me, I hope,' said the Greek anxiously. 'I try to run my business honestly but sometimes it is difficult.'

'I'm sure it is,' returned Biggles dryly, as he went out into the street. 'I don't think you have anything to worry about.'

'What do you make of him?' asked Ginger, as they walked away.

'He's all right,' answered Biggles. 'Anyway, as right as a dealer can be in this part of the world. He must meet some shady customers. I'm pretty sure he didn't know where those pearls had come from, but he suspected they were "hot" and wouldn't touch 'em. That says something for his principles as well as his common sense, for it must have been a great temptation. It could also be true that he couldn't afford to buy the lot, anyway, even if Bowden was prepared to sell, for the whole collection must be worth a million. Well, now we know that our theory about Bowden wasn't far wrong we'll push along to Paris. These coasting vessels are mostly slow so we should be in the Rue de la Paix before him.'

Said Ginger, 'I'm looking forward to the pleasure of seeing Bowden's face when he finds us waiting for him.'

'Remind me when we refuel at Alexandria to send a cable to Marcel, at the Sûreté, asking him to meet us at Le Bourget. As we can't make arrests in France we shall need his help. I'll ask him, too, to find out when this boat, the *Charbonniere,* is due at Marseilles.'

'You won't meet the boat there?'

'No. He's bound to go on to Paris, and I imagine he won't waste any time. He'll want to be rid of those pearls as quickly as possible. Even if he doesn't go straight to Paris he'll be somewhere in France and it shouldn't take the French police long to find him. He won't be expecting trouble.'

'If I know anything he'll spend the rest of his life wondering where his scheme came unstuck,' opined Ginger. 'It was all so simple, and so beautifully worked out, that even now I'm not sure where it went wrong.'

'His one mistake was in buying an aircraft for a job it couldn't possibly do,' averred Biggles. 'It may have been the best type for the purpose for which he really wanted it, which was a night landing in Arabia, but not for the purpose for which he said he wanted it – the Cape record. But let's get along.'

Marcel was waiting on the tarmac when the Proctor landed at the Paris airport.

'What now, old dog,' he greeted, cheerfully. 'From the colour of your face you have been where the sun shines.'

'As you had a cable from me from Egypt you knew that before you saw my face, so don't swank your detective stuff on me,' chaffed Biggles. 'What about the boat I mentioned, the *Charbonniere*? Have you found out where she is?'

'But certainly. She docks at Marseilles this morning.'

'Good. That should give me time to tell you what this is about before we proceed to business. Let's go to the buffet and have something to eat. We've nearly lived in the air for the past ten days, without regular meals, and I'm beginning to feel like a wet bus ticket.'

At a table in a quiet corner of the refreshment-room Biggles gave his French colleague of the International Police Bureau the main facts of the case that had caused him to spend so much time in the air. 'If I thought Bowden would go on to England I'd nab him there, but he may not,' he concluded. 'With money in his pocket he may stay in France, or for that matter, go anywhere.'

'It would be safer to finish the business here,' declared Marcel. 'If you want him in England there should be no difficulty about an extradition order when we have this clever gentleman in the bag, as you call it. When you have finished eating like a starved dog let us go and see Monsieur Corton, of Corton et Cie. They are a big firm, very sound, and he will do whatever I ask. They have the best pearls in the world.'

Presently a taxi took them to the famous Paris street of jewellers, and Marcel having presented his card at their destination, they were promptly shown into the office of the managing director, Monsieur Corton, senior. Having accepted an invitation to be seated, Biggles, at Marcel's request, explained the situation.

'What would you like me to do?' inquired Monsieur Corton.

Biggles laid on the desk the inventory and description of the stolen pearls. 'If Bowden arrives here with pearls we can be sure of where he got them, but we must not make a mistake,' he said. 'This is my suggestion. When Bowden arrives, say that you will buy the pearls, but in view of their unusual quality it will take a little while to value them.'

'That would happen in any case,' asserted the Frenchman.

'You can either ask Bowden to wait, or call back later at a time arranged. In his absence you will check the pearls to confirm that they are in fact those that were stolen. Should that be so you will telephone Monsieur Brissac at Police Headquarters where we shall be waiting. Not knowing exactly when Bowden will arrive we cannot stay here all day, and perhaps tomorrow as well, to interrupt your work. On receipt of your message we will come straight here, arrest the man and take him away.'

Monsieur Corton bowed. '*Bien entendu*. It shall be as you say.'

'*Merci bien, monsieur.*'

With that they left and went to Marcel's office, there to await what they could confidently expect to be the last act of the drama.

Biggles thought it unlikely that Bowden would present his note from the Greek until the following day, but in that he was wrong. It may be that, as Biggles had predicted, Bowden was anxious to be rid of the pearls with the least possible delay, as in the circumstances would be understandable. At all events, shortly after three o'clock Marcel's phone jangled, and the famous jeweller informed him that the wanted man had called. He had gone away, and would return at five precisely to complete the sale if the valuation was agreed. The pearls, stated Monsieur Corton, were those described in the book of the late Sheikh Ibn Usfa.

'That's all we need to know,' Biggles told Marcel. 'We'll be there to receive the gentleman.' .

'I will take two of my best men along in case he objects, as no doubt he will as the charge will be murder,' said Marcel. 'I do not like fighting with fists.'

'He has a gun,' warned Biggles, 'and if I know the type he'll use it. I want that gun. It should be a useful piece of evidence, for in my pocket is the bullet that killed his partner, Renford. The Sheikh was killed with the same weapon, no doubt.'

A few minutes before five o'clock found them with the jeweller in his private office, making the final arrangements. With them Marcel had brought two plain-clothes gendarmes. These were posted in strategic positions as if they might have been customers, or shop assistants. Marcel was also in plain clothes.

'I would like to have it from Bowden's own lips, before witnesses, that the pearls are his,' Biggles told Monsieur Corton. 'You would oblige me, therefore, if you would put the question to him.'

'I will do that,' was the reply.

'You might also, as a matter of interest, ask him how the pearls came into his possession. No doubt he will have anticipated that question and have the answer ready. I should like to know what it is.'

'Certainly, monsieur. It shall be as you say.'

With that they took up positions about the room in order that the trap should not appear too obvious.

They had not long to wait.

A few minutes after five there came a knock on the door. At the jeweller's invitation it was opened by the shop manager, who had been taken into their confidence, to admit Bowden. He had shaved off his moustache, but Ginger, who had seen his photograph, recognized him nevertheless.

'Come right in, monsieur,' requested Corton, who was seated at his desk.

'You've looked at the pearls?' queried Bowden, advancing.

'Yes, they are a very fine lot, so fine that they excite my curiosity,' answered Corton. 'May I ask where you got them?'

'Does that matter?'

Corton made a little gesture. 'We have to be careful you know, particularly with new clients. You will appreciate that.'

'Of course.'

'These pearls are really yours?'

'Definitely.'

'You haven't told me yet where they came from.'

'I picked them up one at a time while I was trading along the Malabar Coast.'

'Strange. Pearls being my business I would have said they came out of the Red Sea,' observed Corton.

There he may have gone a little too far.

Suspicion flashed into Bowden's eyes. 'If you don't want them give me them back,' he said shortly. At the same time he took a swift glance round the room, and it so happened that at the same moment Biggles turned towards him.

What followed happened with such speed that the police were all caught, as Biggles afterwards put it, on one foot. It had been confidently expected that Bowden would be so taken by surprise that the arrest would be easy. But it did not happen like that. As Bowden's eyes met those of Biggles his face turned ashen, and the only explanation of his conduct was that he not only recognized him but knew of his position in the Air Police, which was a possibility Biggles had not taken into account, although he confessed later that he should have done since Bowden had been employed at Gatwick, where the Air Police had their operational headquarters.

Be that as it may, Bowden's air-trained ability to think fast now made itself apparent. That he had suddenly grasped the situation was evident, for he turned in a flash, and hurling aside Marcel as he jumped forward to stop him, reached the door. This he flung open with such force that the two gendarmes who had been standing by it were sent staggering back. Bowden dashed between them, and dodging through the customers in the shop, reached the street.

Biggles and Ginger were hot on his heels, but were hindered by having the swing door flung back in their faces. By the time they had recovered, and were through, Bowden was half-way across the street, twisting and dodging through the traffic, regardless of screaming brakes, wailing sirens and shouts.

'We've lost him,' thought Ginger, as he started to follow, to be missed by inches by a taxi. Indeed, for a moment it looked certain that Bowden would escape.

Suddenly the traffic had stopped. There was a significant hush. A woman screamed.

Ginger did not see exactly what happened, for a van had pulled up between him and the fugitive. But he saw men jumping from their vehicles and guessed the truth. By the time he was round the van he could see it. Bowden was under the wheels of a lorry in which a white-faced driver sat gesticulating wildly at the several people who were telling him what to do – go forward, go back, or remain still.

Ginger joined Biggles in the middle of the road. Marcel came to them. None of them spoke. There was really nothing to say.

Presently, Marcel moved forward to a uniformed point-duty gendarme who had pushed through the fast-collecting crowd. 'How badly is he hurt?' he asked.

'He's dead,' said someone. 'The wheels went over him. I saw it all. The man must have been mad.'

An ambulance announced its approach in the usual French fashion, with wailing horn.

Biggles looked at Marcel. 'What a mess,' he muttered. 'What do you want us to do?'

'There is nothing you can do,' answered Marcel. 'You had better leave this to me. I will attend to everything.'

'Thanks,' acknowledged Biggles. 'In that case I'll push along home to tell my chief what has happened. I'll come back later. Meantime, there are one or two things you can do for me. Collect the pearls from Monsieur Corton, also the little book, the inventory, I left with him. As soon as I've had a rest I'll take them back to where they belong. Oh, and by the way, I think you'll find a revolver in Bowden's pocket. If the man's dead we shan't need it for evidence, but I'd like to have it to check up on the bullet that killed Renford, for our records.'

'I will do all this,' promised Marcel.

'Fine. Then I'll leave you to it. See you later.' Biggles turned and walked away.

'Bowden must have been crazy to act like that,' remarked Ginger as, in a taxi, they headed for the airport.

'It was his only chance of getting away and he took it. He jolly nearly got away with it, too,' said Biggles ruefully. 'After all, he had nothing to lose except his life and he'd probably have lost that, anyway. We had a clear case against him. He must have known me by sight. I didn't take that possibility into account. But there, one can't think of everything.'

'You thought of enough to tidy up a cold-blooded murder, if ever there was one, that nearly went on the records as accidental death – and the death of the wrong man, at that.'

'Which all goes to show that one can't be sure of anything, not even death,' returned Biggles tritely. 'If ever there was a cunningly contrived murder – two murders, in fact – this was it.'

'And but for a fluke it would have come off,' said Ginger.

'I wouldn't call it a fluke, exactly,' replied Biggles. 'Say, rather, the thing came to light because the murderer made a mistake, his mistake being the choice of an aircraft for a job it couldn't possibly do. Fortunately, most murderers make a blunder. That's why they so seldom get away with it.'

'And to think it all began with a forced landing. The Sheikh offered Bowden hospitality. Bowden saw the pearls –'

'And I'd say he's been wondering ever since how he could get his hands on them,' concluded Biggles.

'After we've tidied up at this end we'll fly them back to the new sheikh, and do our best to explain that all officers are not like this scoundrel Bowden, otherwise anyone else having a forced landing on that coast is liable to have a thin time.'

2

THE MAN
WHO LOST HIS FOOT

BIGGLES looked up from his desk as the door of the
Air Police office opened and a man walked in. His face
was thin and chalky white, and in it his eyes looked
unnaturally large and bright. His lips quivered as he
said: 'Hello, Biggles.'

Staring, Biggles half rose and sank down again. 'Am
I supposed to know you?' he asked.

'Of course you know me. I'm Nobby Donovan of
241 Squadron.'

Biggles' eyes opened wide. 'Sorry. I wouldn't have
known you. What on earth have you been doing to
yourself?'

'That's what I've come to tell you, old man.'

Biggles glanced at Ginger. 'Get him a chair.'

Ginger pulled one forward.

The ex-pilot slumped into it. 'Do you know what
I'm going to do?'

'Give me a clue.'

'I'm going to bash a brick through a jeweller's
window. Actually, I was on my way to do it when I
remembered you and what you were doing nowadays;

so I thought I'd drop in and tell you to have a black van handy.'

'Is throwing bricks through windows a new pastime you've discovered?'

'No. This will be the first time.'

'What's the idea?'

'I want to go to prison. How long will I get, do you think?'

'What you want,' returned Biggles slowly, 'is a hospital. Why a prison?'

'It's the only way I can think of to get myself cured.'

'Of what?'

'I'm a dope fiend.'

Biggles offered his cigarette case, the drug addict took one with fingers that so trembled that he dropped it. 'How did this unholy habit start?' asked Biggles.

'By accident, I assure you. Don't be too hard on me. It's hell, and the only way I can get any comfort is to stay there. You may not remember but I was hit in the Battle of Britain. They had to take my foot off and give me an artificial one. From that time I've suffered from the pain people sometimes get after an amputation. Sounds silly, I know, but the pain is in the foot I haven't got. But the nerve that runs from the foot to the brain is still there, so from time to time it reminds you of what you've lost. That's what the doctors say. They gave me some pills to take the edge off the agony. They helped a bit.'

'They weren't responsible for your present condition.'

'Oh no. That came about like this, and I think it could have happened to anyone. One day I was out on my job – which I've since lost, by the way – when the pain got me. I was in agony. I had no pills on me so I popped into a chemist's to see if he could do anything about it. He said he thought he could – in fact, I couldn't have gone to a better place.'

'What did he do?'

'He gave me some white powder. It was miraculous. It acted like a charm. For the first time for years I was really free from pain. You fellows who are always fit don't realize what that means. The stuff was expensive. He charged me three quid, which I thought was a bit steep, and said so. But I had to admit the relief was worth it.'

'Did you ask him the name of this stuff?'

'No. I was only too thankful that the pain had gone.'

'But you know now.'

'I think so. From what I've read since I'm pretty sure it must be heroin.'

Biggles nodded. 'That was my guess. Carry on.'

'Naturally, the next time I got the pain I went flat out for what seemed like a miracle cure. And so it went on. You can guess the rest. By the time the first suspicion hit me that the stuff was dope I had caught the habit, and you don't need me to tell you what that means. I just had to have the stuff. It's all very well for people who have never been in pain to talk about giving up a drug, but let them try it. The crafty devil who was supplying the stuff knew all about that, so he raised the price. Said it was hard to get.'

'That was probably true, anyway,' put in Biggles.

'Well, the long and short of it is, he's now had every penny I possessed. I'm flat broke and going out of my mind. I realize he was never afraid of my giving him away because if I did I'd cut off the supply.'

'I gather he won't let you have any more.'

'He would if I had the money to pay for it. He reckons, of course, that I'll get the money from somewhere. That's where he's wrong. I've come to the end of my tether. This is the pay-off.'

'Who is this nasty piece of work and where does he hang out?' inquired Biggles.

'His name is Valesid. I imagine he's a Greek. Runs a little chemist's shop in a back street near Paddington station. You can see for yourself what he's done to me. It frightens me to look in a mirror. This morning I made a resolution, which was to put myself where I *couldn't* get the stuff. Hence the going to prison idea.'

'You're not the first man to have that idea,' replied Biggles, dryly. 'But there are less uncomfortable ways of putting yourself beyond reach of temptation. But before we come to that let's get this straight. You didn't by any chance come to see me hoping I'd give you money so that you could make a bee-line for Paddington –'

'No,' broke in Donovan. 'Definitely not. I'll take my oath –'

'All right, all right; I'll take your word for it. Just a minute.' Biggles picked up a newspaper and turned the pages, studying the advertisements. 'There's a cargo boat leaving in the morning for Fremantle, Western Australia, with a few cabins vacant. It'll take you six weeks to get there. You won't find any dope on the ship and if you can hold out for six weeks you'll be cured. I'll buy you a ticket if you'll swear not to step off the ship at any intermediate port.'

'I'll accept that and repay you from the first money I earn.'

'You'll have a tough time.'

'If I can't stick it I can always jump overboard.'

'Fair enough. I'll fix it. Now for one or two questions. Can you tell me any more about this dope shop?'

'Not much, the little swipe is as tight as an oyster. Has to be, I suppose. But I have an idea the dope reaches him in a Rolls-Royce, and I'll tell you why. Twice I've seen a Rolls pull up and a woman get out. She has a uniformed chauffeur, a colored man who looks as if he might be an Egyptian. The dame herself is dark and well-dressed; maybe a bit too well-dressed. Naturally I took her to be another customer. Then one day when I called Valesid was out of stock. He told me to come back in half an hour. I was in such a state I paced up and down. Then the Rolls came. When it had gone I went in, and it was okay. He had the stuff.'

'Did you take the number of this car?'

'No. I didn't think of it at the time.'

'No matter. We'll get it. Tell me, why didn't you report this to the police earlier?'

'For two reasons. The first is obvious. Had the police grabbed Valesid I would have cut off my supplies. Secondly, he told me that if I squealed the gang would get me. That could be true, because I often saw sinister dago-looking types hanging about. That's all.'

'Okay,' said Biggles. 'I'm not letting you out of sight till the ship sails. Algy, go with him, get the ticket, give him some lunch and then take him to the flat and stay there.'

'Okay,' said Algy, quietly. 'Come on, Donovan.' They went out.

Biggles shook his head as he watched them go.

As the door closed behind them Ginger said: 'It seems fantastic that a man of his calibre can't break himself of a habit.'

'Of all narcotics heroin is probably the worst,' answered Biggles. 'It not only destroys a man's body but his soul. Habit? Addicts who have had the drug withheld have been known to go out of their minds. What about cigarettes? Nicotine is a mild narcotic, and like the rest is habit-forming. Every time the price of cigarettes goes up thousands of people give up smoking. Can they stick it? No. Within a week or two most of them are smoking again. Multiply the smoking habit a hundred times and you'll get an idea of what a grip a real drug gets on you. In spite of severe penalties drugs have rotted the entire Middle East, which is the centre of the dope racket. The trouble about stopping it is the enormous profits hanging to the traffic. A pound weight of heroin, costing only a matter of shillings to manufacture, can retail at four or five hundred pounds. At one time certain European countries were not above dipping a finger in this profitable pie.'

'What is this stuff heroin, anyway?'

'Heroin is an alkaloid derived from the opium poppy. The coagulated juice taken from the seed-pod is opium. Treated with certain chemicals it becomes morphine. Treated again with anhydride of acetic acid it is converted into a white powder, diacetyl morphine, otherwise heroin.'

'So all you need to get it is to grow the right sort of poppy,' put in Bertie Lissie.

'Correct. This particular poppy is a plant with grey-green foliage and single mauve flowers. The best comes from the high ground in Asia Minor. The question we're faced with now is, how is it coming into the country? I think I'll have a word with Inspector Gaskin. He'll have to know about this sooner or later.'

Biggles called the Inspector's office and asked him to come up.

The detective came. Biggles told him the story.

'What do you want me to do – pick up this dope pedlar?' asked the Inspector, when he had finished.

'And let the big shot get away? Not likely. That shop at Paddington won't be the only one. When we strike we've got to nail the lot. My angle will be to find out how the stuff is being imported. What I'd like you to do is work on the Rolls. You'll spot it if you watch the shop. Who owns it? Mark where it goes. You'll have to be careful, or at the first sniff that they're being trailed they'll vanish – or the dope will. When you've got the gen come and have another word with me.'

'Okay.' The C.I.D. Inspector departed.

For a week nothing was seen of him. Then he walked in. 'We're all set if you're ready to go,' he announced.

'Do you know how the stuff's getting into the country?' asked Biggles.

'No. Do you?'

'No. Yet every port, sea and air, has been alerted. Until we have that information we're not ready to go anywhere, because whatever else we do the stuff will continue to arrive. What have you been able to find out?'

Gaskin filled his pipe, slowly and methodically. 'The

Rolls belongs to an Egyptian–Greek named Arbram
Nifar. Got a house in Hill Street, Mayfair. He's a
high-class Turkish and Egyptian cigarette importer –
in a small way, I'd say, since he doesn't seem to handle
any of the known brands. Still, he seems to do himself
pretty well. His wife does most of the running about.
She's got an Egyptian chauffeur whom she calls Ali,
and seems to be on good terms with some of the wide
boys who drift around the West End night clubs apparently living on air. We've traced the car to shops in
Paddington, Soho, Limehouse and Mayfair. These
four seem to be the lot. Nifar and his wife spend the
week-ends out of Town. Seems they've got a farm in
Devon. Probably one of these tax-dodging set-ups. I
can't imagine him farming for any other reason.'

'Unless the farm comes into the dope racket,' suggested Biggles. 'It could be to that address the importer delivers the stuff. He may think a London house
is too dangerous.'

'That could be the answer,' murmured Gaskin.

'I think we ought to have a look at this farm before
we show our hand. It must come into the racket some-
how.'

'Or we could grab the car on its way back to Town.'

'We'd look silly if we struck an occasion when there
was nothing in it. We ought to be sure of ourselves
before we pounce.'

'That risk is always on the boards whatever we do,'
averred the Inspector. 'I don't suppose these crooks
leave the stuff lying about on the sideboard, either in
Devon or in London.'

'That's why I feel we should know where it starts
from before we try picking it up *en route*. Leave it for

a day or two. I'll run down to Devon and cast an eye over this farm from ground level.'

'Okay, if that's how you prefer it. There's no hurry as far as I'm concerned.' Gaskin nodded and went out.

'Bring the car round, Ginger,' ordered Biggles. 'We'll give ourselves a spot of fresh air if nothing else.'

'Right away?'

'Yes.'

'What's the hurry?'

'Because today's Saturday. You heard what Gaskin said about this cigarette importer and his wife spending the week-end on their country farm. They go on Saturday and return on Monday. That strikes me as the best time to make a reconnaissance. For which reason you'd better come along. Algy, and you, Bertie. If this farm is any size there will be a lot of ground to cover.'

It was late in the afternoon when the police car cruised through the quiet Devon village that was the postal address of Nifar's farm. A boy directed them to it and they were soon moving slowly down one of those sunken roads so common in the county. With the banks ten or twelve feet high nothing could be seen beyond the hedges that topped them.

'This is no use,' observed Biggles, bringing the car to a halt. 'Slip out, Ginger, and cast an eye around from the top.'

Ginger got out and scrambled up the bank. He was soon back. 'It's a field of beans,' he announced. 'I can't see anything else because a barbed wire fence runs round the perimeter.'

They went on two hundred yards and tried again, with the same result.

'Can't you see any cattle?' asked Biggles.

'No. It's the same beanfield.'

'Why does he want a barbed wire fence round a beanfield?'

Nobody answered.

Biggles drove on, but slowed to a stop when an entrance gate appeared. A farm cottage stood on one side of it. A coloured man was working in the garden. He dropped his spade and came forward quickly as Biggles got out and advanced towards the gate. 'This is a private road,' he said shortly, with a thick foreign accent.

'I can see that,' answered Biggles evenly. 'Can you tell me if I'm on the right road for Moreton Hampstead?'

'Not know. I am stranger here.'

'Thanks,' acknowledged Biggles. He returned to the car and drove on.

'He wasn't letting anyone inside,' said Ginger.

'That, I imagine, is why he's there,' replied Biggles dryly.

He drove on for some way, the sunken lane persisting. From time to time he stopped, but only once could Ginger report that he could see a house and some farm buildings in the distance. Always the barbed wire fence was there.

'We're nearly back to where we started from,' said Biggles. 'We've been all round the place. There's only one entrance and a man is guarding it. As I don't want him to see us again for fear we make him suspicious we might as well go home.'

'Home! Do you mean to London?' asked Algy, looking surprised.

'I do. If we can't get a dekko at this establishment from floor level, tomorrow we'll see what it looks like from up topsides. We'll bring a camera, too, and then if necessary we shall be able to study the place at our leisure.'

A minute later Biggles had to pull in tight against the bank to allow a Rolls-Royce to pass.

'So they've arrived,' he observed. 'It gives me an idea. As there's only one entrance to the farm anyone arriving with a parcel of dope will have to use it. Algy, I'm going to drop you and Bertie off to keep an eye on that gate until we rejoin you tomorrow. All you have to do is watch the gate, keeping out of sight, and note anyone who comes or goes. Devon suggests that the stuff may be leaking through one of the county's several ports, so don't be surprised if you see a man looking as though he might be a sailor. There's also a chance, of course, that the Rolls may go out to collect the stuff. In any case one of you will ring me at the flat at six o'clock tomorrow morning to give me the gen. There's a phone box in the village. As long as one of you remains on watch the other can fetch enough food to tide you over until we come back.'

'Okay,' agreed Algy.

The car returned to London without incident.

At six the following morning the phone in Biggles' room rang. Waiting for the call he picked up the receiver, listened for a minute or two, and then said: 'Okay. We're on our way.' He hung up.

Turning to Ginger he remarked, 'That's odd. Algy

says not a soul has entered or left the place. I felt sure they'd see someone during the night. Queer.' He shrugged. 'Maybe this isn't the week for the stuff to arrive.'

'It could be the Rolls goes down on the off-chance that it might,' offered Ginger.

'True enough,' agreed Biggles. 'No matter. We'll carry on as arranged. Let's get cracking.'

Two hours later, at the controls of a police Proctor aircraft he was flying a straight course over the farm of which so little could be seen from the road. Now everything was in plain view, and Ginger was soon busy with the camera, concentrating on a large house with several outbuildings that stood surrounded by fields of crops. No cattle or horses were to be seen.

'There's your beanfield,' observed Biggles casually. 'Our jolly farmer friends must fairly dote on beans. There must be twenty acres of them.' He broke off, and then went on in a different voice. 'No. It couldn't be.'

'Couldn't be what?'

'Take a good look at the beanfield. You'll notice two pale stripes running across it. They stop well inside the field on both sides. There are some men working in them.'

'What about them?'

'What do you make those stripes to be?'

'It's hard to say from here.'

'Have you ever seen anything quite like them before?'

'No. I can't say I have. They look like flowers of some sort. I believe they raise flowers in this part of the world for the London markets.'

'Spring flowers. What sort of flowers would growers raise in the summer and why put them in the middle of a beanfield?'

'You tell me,' said Ginger, helplessly. 'I haven't a clue.'

'You'll think I'm crazy, and I may be, but the only place I've seen crops looking like that is in the Middle East, where the farmers have a reason for growing certain flowers where they can't be seen – and the middle of another crop is as good a place as any. Well – well – well. Would you believe it! No wonder Algy saw no one. How wrong I was in supposing that this Devon set-up was in order to be near the sea. There was a better reason than that.'

'What was it?'

'The climate – the mild climate which produces the early spring flowers.'

Suddenly Ginger got it. 'You don't mean those stripes down there are – poppies!'

'Considering what we know, and for want of any other explanation, that's what they look like to me, fantastic though it may seem.'

'How are you going to confirm it? Are you going down?'

'Not on your life. If I did, the people below would guess why, and scuttle like rabbits when a ferret pops in. We'll get home and come back after dark properly equipped for the job. Blow me down and pick me up, as Bertie would say. An opium farm right on our doorstep. No wonder the Customs people were baffled. For sheer brass face this is the tops.'

While he had been speaking Biggles had made a wide turn and was now heading east. 'The thing's so hard to believe that we shall have to make sure we're not barking up the wrong tree,' he went on. 'A visit to the botanical gardens at Kew seems indicated.'

'By properly equipped I take it you mean wire-cutters,' said Ginger.

'No. Should that fence be patrolled a gap in the wire would be seen; and that, in an establishment that seems to be protected like an atomic station, would be enough to set the pigeons flying. A couple of stiff rugs thrown over the wire will enable us to get over it without tearing ourselves to pieces, and without leaving a mark.'

In rather more than an hour the Proctor was back at its base, and within a few minutes, again in the car with a roll of doped aeroplane fabric on the back seat, they were on their way to Kew. It was Sunday, but as Biggles pointed out, that being a popular day in the Gardens, there was all the more reason to suppose an official would be on duty.

This turned out to be the case, and at the offices of the Royal Horticultural Society they were taken to the room of an assistant secretary, who asked what he could do for them. His eyebrows went up when Biggles introduced himself and showed his police pass.

'I have come to ask you if you happen to have here a specimen of the opium poppy,' began Biggles. 'If so, I'd like to refresh my memory with a sight of it.'

The secretary smiled. 'Had you been anyone but a police officer I would have hesitated to say yes, because it's not a plant we would encourage the public to grow. However, come with me and I will show you *Papaver Somniferum*, to give it its botanical name.'

'I take it, then, the plant would grow in this country?' questioned Biggles.

'Certainly.'

'In the open?'

'Yes.'

As they looked at the plant the secretary said: 'Are you interested in the flower or in its rather sinister by-product?'

'I'm interested in the possible production of opium in this country,' returned Biggles, frankly.

'No doubt a warmer climate would be more likely to produce a higher opium content than a cold one. The drug, as you probably know, is derived from the seed pod, or rather, the sap that oozes from it when it is scratched, and I imagine it would flow more freely in a warm place than a cold one.'

'You think the plant would thrive in Devonshire, for instance?'

'I see no reason why it shouldn't.'

'Thank you,' acknowledged Biggles. 'That's really all I wanted to know.'

It was late in the afternoon when the car arrived back at the Devon rendezvous, where, as there was no longer any point in Algy and Bertie continuing their task, they were relieved and taken to the village inn for a substantial high tea. They still had nothing to report, so Biggles told them the result of his day's work.

'Sizzling sausages!' exclaimed Bertie. 'What will people get up to next?'

'If opium is as easy as that to produce, the wonder is that no one has tried it before,' said Algy. 'What beats me is how you got on to it so quickly.'

'That was merely a matter of that useful thing called experience,' answered Biggles. 'When I saw those stripes in the beanfield it touched off a chord in my memory. Years ago, when the R.A.F. was in Egypt, although I never did the job myself, there was a regular patrol on the look-out for poppies, the growing of which was illegal. At first ground forces handled it. But the culprits got over that by growing small patches of the stuff in the middle of ordinary crops. These couldn't be seen from the ground but they were plain enough to see from the air. Maybe the fact that the crop here was beans had something to do with my remembering what I'd heard in the Middle East, because there it was usually in a beanfield that the stuff was spotted. Beans grow to about the same height as poppies. Anyway, there it is. According to Gaskin Nifar is an Egyptian, so he'd know all about it. On the face of it you might think he had a nerve to grow poppies here; but how many people would see them, and of those, how many would suspect their purpose? I happen to be one of those who could guess the answer.'

'And what's the next move?' asked Algy.

'Obviously, the next move is to prove what at present we only suspect, and the only way to do that is to get a sample of what Nifar is growing in his bean-field. There were some men working there this morning, and if my guess is right they were Egyptians collecting that infernal juice. It's a job for an expert. The local people wouldn't know how to do it. Besides it would be dangerous to ask them. They'd talk, and the village constable might well wonder what was going on. We'll make a sortie over that barbed wire

fence as soon as it's dark. I've brought some fabric
to throw over it, to save tearing ourselves, and our
clothes, to pieces.'

'And if these posies turn out to be opium poppies,
what then, old boy?' put in Bertie.

Biggles thought for a moment. 'The particular dope
we're dealing with isn't opium, although that may
come into the picture. Donovan was getting heroin,
which is worse, and has to be manufactured. The stuff
may be produced here, or in London, although I'd say
here, in one of the outbuildings. Either way, opium or
heroin, when Nifar and his wife return to London, we
can reckon they take some with them.'

'Then you won't grab them here, at the farm?' Algy
spoke.

'No. That would mean bringing in the county police
and time would be lost in explanations. We can clean
up here after we've dealt with the agents who distri-
bute the stuff in London. When we've checked that the
plants are what I think they are we'll get back to Town
and leave Gaskin and his plain-clothes men to do the
mopping up. The thing is to get the whole gang into
the bag with one cast of the net. Nothing we do pleases
me more than to jump on these drug traffickers. Every
one of 'em is a potential murderer – a slow murderer
of the vilest kind.'

They killed time until sundown and then made their
way quietly and without haste to that part of the lane
which Biggles knew from his air reconnaissance was
nearest to the sinister stripes that had first aroused his
suspicions.

With Ginger carrying the roll of fabric he got
out.

'Turn the car and wait for us here,' he told Algy. 'We shouldn't be many minutes.'

The car glided on into the fast gathering darkness.

Having climbed up the bank Biggles took the fabric and having folded it treble thickness arranged it on the barbed wire fence. In a matter of seconds they were over it, without injury to themselves or their clothes.

'Walk up one of the drills,' ordered Biggles softly. 'We mustn't knock flat more beans than can be prevented in case there's an inspection every morning.'

They had taken only a few paces when Ginger stumbled and nearly fell.

'What are you doing?' asked Biggles irritably.

'I tripped over something,' explained Ginger.

Simultaneously, from no great distance away, came the barking of dogs.

Biggles took a pace back and groped for the object over which Ginger had tripped. 'It's a wire,' he muttered. 'That must have set off an alarm. Come on. Speed is the thing now.'

They hurried on towards the objective, now appearing in the gloom as a pale grey streak. At the same time the dogs were clearly coming nearer, and from the noise they made they were obviously not mere terriers. Biggles did not speak. Working swiftly with his knife he slashed through one of the plants near the root, and as this was all he needed he turned at once for the fence, breaking into a run.

Haste, though necessary, was nearly their undoing, for in the dark, and they dare not use torches, they struck the fence at a point below the fabric, and by the time they had corrected their mistake the heavy panting of the dogs, no longer barking, could be heard coming down the wire. In fact, two mastiffs rushed up, snarling, while Biggles was removing the fabric, and such was the fury of their attack that Ginger rolled down the bank into the road. Biggles followed with more haste than dignity, for the animals could be heard throwing themselves against the fence in an effort to break through it, and there was reason to suppose that at any moment they might jump over it. Fortunately at that moment the car glided up.

'Keep going,' ordered Biggles tersely, as they tumbled in.

'You seem to have started something, old boy,' remarked Bertie, as the car shot forward.

'Are you telling me!' panted Ginger. 'The bally place is guarded like a fortress. Trip wires, dogs, and what have you.'

'Nifar had good reason to discourage trespassers,' said Biggles. 'No matter. I have one of his poppies.'

'He'll know someone has been in the field,' said Algy.

'He may think the alarm was caused by a poacher,' speculated Biggles. 'Why not? I imagine they have poachers here as well as most other places. He has no reason to suspect the truth, anyhow. Stop when you reach the village, Algy. I'm anxious to have a look at this bunch of flowers I'm carrying.'

When the car ran to a halt against a village lamp-post he examined the plant he had cut in the field.

'This is it,' he declared. 'Take a look at that,' he went on, pointing out some cuts in a seed pod from which a white latex still oozed. 'That's what those fellows were doing in the field. Harvesting the dope. It's all we need to know.'

'Nifar might take fright and bolt, after that alarm,' said Algy.

'Even if he does he's almost certain to make for his London house,' asserted Biggles.

'His car may be faster than ours,' Algy pointed out. 'If he started right away he could be there before us.'

'That's true,' agreed Biggles. 'We can easily make allowances for that. I'll ring Gaskin and tell him what's cooking. He'll do what's necessary. I might as well do it from here. Wait for me.'

Biggles got out and walked on to the call-box outside the village post office.

He was away about ten minutes. When he came back he was smiling.

'I had a job to make Gaskin believe I wasn't fooling,' he explained. 'A dope factory in Devon does sound a bit far-fetched, I must admit. So do a lot of things these days, if it comes to that. Let's push on home. There's no particular hurry. Gaskin says he'll have everything under control long before we're there.'

What Arbram Nifar and his wife thought about the night alarm in Devon, if they thought about it at all, was never known, but it may be supposed that, judging from their behaviour, they did not take it seriously. It could be that their unique scheme for producing drugs in England had for so long been successful that they had grown careless – a state of mind by no means uncommon in those who break the law.

At all events, they must have stayed on at the farm until late the next morning, for the Rolls did not arrive back at the house in Mayfair until its usual hour. This gave Biggles, with Inspector Gaskin and some of his men, ample time to perfect their plan for a complete round-up of the gang, and take up their positions accordingly. In short, when the Rolls drew up at the door of Nifar's residence Biggles and Inspector Gaskin were watching from a plain van a few yards higher up the street. This, Biggles had asserted, was for several reasons a more satisfactory scheme than stopping the car somewhere on the road.

Nifar's coloured chauffeur jumped out smartly and opening the rear door took out two small suitcases. With these in his hands he advanced to the door of the house, followed closely by his employers. Nifar took out his latch-key and put it in the door, but before this could be opened the police were on the step beside him.

'Just a moment, sir,' said Gaskin quietly.

'What – what is this?' blustered Nifar, his dark eyes darting glances from Gaskin to Biggles.

Actually, he must have known the answer to his question, for the colour had drained from his face, leaving it ghastly under its brown skin.

'We're police officers, and I must ask you to show me the contents of those suitcases,' said Gaskin politely, but with cold deliberation.

The woman screamed.

'Instead of making a scene in the street suppose we go inside,' suggested Gaskin imperturbably. 'It will be better for everyone that way.'

Moving like a man in a dream Nifar unlocked the door and pushed it open. They all moved on into the hall.

'Now,' went on Gaskin. 'Let's have a look in these bags.'

The suitcases were locked. The Inspector held out a hand. 'The keys,'please.'

Nifar, with a shaking hand, passed them over. 'These – these cases aren't mine,' he stammered.

'Whose are they?' demanded Gaskin evenly.

'They belong to a friend of mine.'

'Do you know what's in them?'

'Er – no.'

'Then why get so upset?'

By this time Biggles had put the cases on the hall table, unlocked them and thrown back the lids to reveal the contents. These were not quite what he expected, consisting of a number of small, neat, brown-paper parcels. Some carried a name only, others an address as well, as if intended for posting.

A slow smile spread over Gaskin's face as he picked up one or two of the packages and read the inscriptions. 'Well – well – well,' he murmured softly. 'This is the best thing that has happened in this country for a long time.' He cocked an eye at Biggles. 'I've been waiting quite a while to learn how some of these smart guys live in luxury without working. Now we know. What a haul!'

'We'd better have a look at one of these parcels, to make sure,' suggested Biggles.

'Go ahead.'

While Biggles was opening a package picked up at random the Inspector turned to Nifar. 'Do you know what's in these parcels?' he inquired.

The Egyptian, who looked as if he was on the point of collapse, swore in a husky voice that he had no idea.

Said the Inspector calmly: 'Then you'll be as interested as we are to see.'

Biggles disclosed, in neatly folded paper, a quantity of fine white powder.

'Now what have you to say about it?' The Inspector asked Nifar, in a hard voice.

Nifar had nothing to say. Nor had his wife, who slumped in a chair.

Gaskin turned a stern face to the ashen chauffeur. 'If you can see which side your bread is buttered you'll come clean, and do as I tell you. What happens to these parcels without addresses?'

'The people come here for them.'

'Flash Charlie, and Toni, for instance?'

'Yes.'

The Inspector nodded. 'I see. And you go off in the Rolls and deliver the others?'

'Yes.'

'All right. Get on with it. Two of my men will go with you.'

As the chauffeur departed, two plain-clothes men with him, Gaskin looked at Biggles. 'My fellers'll collect these rats as they take delivery. We'll wait here for the others to call.'

And so it worked out. Never was a round-up more complete. As each drug pedlar arrived, and accepted his packet from Nifar, he was arrested by Gaskin's men who, for that purpose, had been placed where they could not be seen. They stepped out when the transaction was completed. Some of the pedlars came in expensive motor-cars, but they all left in the police van.

'Never saw such a lovely collection of spivs in my

life,' said Gaskin with deep satisfaction, at the end of the day, after the last caller had been, and Nifar and his wife had been taken away to complete the party.

Some time later the judge must have thought the same thing, as the gang, which included the foreign workers on the 'farm', appeared before him to receive heavy prison sentences.

'If Nobby Donovan ever gets to hear of this he should reckon he got his own back on a bunch of crooks who nearly drove him to suicide,' opined Ginger, when they were back in the Air Police office.

'I hope he'll think it was worth losing a foot to do the country the best service anyone has done it since the time he lost his,' answered Biggles soberly. 'He should also, now that the dope is no longer available, have solved a problem for a lot of other people who had landed themselves in the same mess as he had.'

3

ASSIGNMENT IN ARABIA

'Good morning, sir.'

' 'Morning, Bigglesworth.' Air Commodore Raymond waved to a chair. 'Sit down. I have a rather unusual job for you.'

Biggles smiled. 'You said that as if most of our jobs were mere routine.'

'I didn't mean it like that. Let us say, this one is a bit more off course than usual.'

Biggles reached for a cigarette. 'All right, sir. Tell me the worst.'

'I want you to fly an Arab boy to an oasis in the Arabian desert.'

'That shouldn't be difficult. But why me? What's wrong with the regular services?'

'If you'll listen I'll tell you why to use the regular air service would defeat its object. This job must be done quietly, secretly and without fuss.'

'Which means, I suppose, that it has a political angle.'

'Correct. Here, in brief, is the story. There is, in the hinterland behind Kuwait, a small province called El Kafala, the Sheikh's residence being an oasis of that name. This sheikh was, until he died a few months ago, a friend of ours; and in order to maintain that friendship it was arranged that his son, now a boy of sixteen, should be educated in this country. That would enable him to learn English and see for himself how a democratic country is run. Well, he came, and was here for nearly three years.'

'You mean, he has gone back?'

'He is back, but he did not go of his own free will. He was abducted. From the speed with which things happened there is good reason to think this boy's father was murdered. At all events, the breath was hardly out of the Sheikh's body when his throne was jumped by a brother – the boy's uncle – a man named Abu Ibn Menzil. He hates us, the reason being that we have always supported his brother, who was without doubt heir to the sheikhdom. You will now begin to see how the land lies.'

'The rightful heir to his father's place was the boy who was in this country, but it has been usurped by his uncle.'

'Exactly. And he has consolidated his position by seizing the boy who is now virtually a prisoner. For this unfortunate state of affairs we were to some extent responsible, for it was while the Foreign Office was considering the best course for this lad to pursue that he was seized, outside his school, and carried home. He is helpless. There is no other claimant but the uncle, who is now in a strong position. He knows perfectly well that we dare not use force to unseat him, for this would cause a flare-up among the more powerful sheikhs in Saudi Arabia, where things are very touchy already, due to the scramble for oil concessions in the region.'

'You know for certain that this boy is back at El Kafala?'

'Yes. The boy, Jerid Beni Menzil is his name, managed to get a letter out by a friend making the pilgrimage to Mecca. He asks for help, and that is a call we cannot ignore.'

'Why hasn't his uncle killed him?'

'That's the point. He will, no doubt, as soon as he feels that his position is assured. What will happen is, it will be given out that Jerid has died of some ailment or other.'

'Why is this uncle so keen on being the Sheikh?'

'Because he looks forward to being a multi-millionaire, as he will be when the oil under his land is tapped. As we don't deal in murder ourselves there can be no question of liquidating this false sheikh. And while the boy is in his hands the less we say the better, for to raise a scream would simply result in Jerid being put to death forthwith. That would be the end of the business as far as we were concerned, for the uncle would then have a legitimate claim to the sheikhdom. In a word, we must get this boy out of his uncle's clutches before we can act.'

'How do the people, the Arabs, feel about this?'

'They would support the boy if he were free. It's unlikely they know where he is. Not knowing he's a prisoner they may be wondering why he doesn't show up.'

'All right. So you want the boy. How are you going to get him?'

'It would, of course, be absurd for you to show your face in El Kafala. Nor could you hope to pass as an Arab. So this is the plan. There is at the London

University a young Arab medical student named Miktel. He knows Jerid, coming from that district. He has been approached and he says he is willing to rescue him if we will take him there. That's where you come in. The idea is, you will fly Miktel to a small oasis some two or three miles from El Kafala, wait there for him, and fly him, and Jerid, back to this country. He will guide you to the oasis.'

'What about landing conditions?'

'He says there are miles and miles of *sabkha* – you know the sort of stuff, mostly gravel – all round the oasis. There's not likely to be anyone there, for at this time of the year the water hole dries out. The place is only visited when the dates are ripe. Well, how do you feel about it?'

'Not entirely happy, but I'll go.'

'When will you be ready to start? There's no time to lose.'

'As soon as this chap Miktel is ready. What about his clothes?'

'He'll be dressed as he would be at home. He has his Arab clothes, *abbas*, *gumbaz*, *kafich*, and so on, with him. He thinks it would be best to arrive about sundown. Leaving you to wait he will go on in the dark. In broad daylight he might be recognized and questioned.'

Biggles got up. 'Okay, sir. I'll get ready. I shall have an opportunity, I suppose, to have a word with this lad Miktel before we start?'

'Of course. Which way will you go?'

Biggles thought for a moment. 'Italy, Cyprus, Amman, and then straight across the Syrian Desert.'

The Air Commodore nodded. 'I'll prepare a

document that should give you diplomatic immunity *en route*. Will you go alone?'

'Yes. The less weight the better. A Proctor would be best for the job, I think. I'll have a reserve machine follow me in case anything should go wrong. These long runs over nothing but sand, in a single-engined job, are always a bit of an anxiety. If anything goes wrong you haven't a hope. It's a comfort to know someone's behind you.'

'All right. Let's call it settled,' concluded the Air Commodore.

On the afternoon of the fifth day after the conversation in the Air Commodore's office an Air Police Proctor aircraft bored a lonely course eastwards from Amman, famous in Biblical history as the capital of the Ammonite kingdom conquered by David, now capital of the Hashemite kingdom of Jordan.

Around the machine the thin desert air quivered under the torture of a merciless sun as it burned its daily journey across a dome of shimmering steel.

Below lay the wilderness, the ancient wilderness of Moab, naked, hopeless, a place of death; a vast area, not of sand in the manner of the Sahara, but of hard baked clay, gravel, ashes, crumbling rocks, pebbles, or a mixture of these things called by the Arab *sabkha*. A land without water.

Always the sun blazed, striking down with lances of white heat, distorting the weary earth into grotesque shapes and making the atmosphere so unstable that the machine sometimes wallowed in 'bumps' of disconcerting violence.

From time to time Biggles, wearing dark glasses as a protection against the glare, glanced at the boy in the seat beside him. Always it was the same, impassive, inscrutable.

Miktel was a fine example of the desert Arab, of medium height, slim, with a flawless olive-brown skin and features of classic regularity. Biggles had come to know the lad well during the past few days, and was aware that behind the mask of imperturbability was courage and a sense of humour. Miktel had told him that he was seventeen, and hoped one day to be a doctor, of which his people were in need.

'Are you feeling all right?' asked Biggles.

'Why not?'

'This sort of bumpy flying sometimes makes people feel sick.'

Miktel flashed one of his quick smiles. 'It is not so bad as riding on a camel for the first time. I am glad I am in the air, for the ground below would burn the soles of my feet after wearing shoes for the pavements of London.'

'You haven't recognized any landmarks yet?'

'No. Nor do I expect to, for this part of the desert is new to me. It looks bad ground after the green fields of England.' Miktel smiled. 'You know, there are still Arabs who believe the English covet our land because it is so much better than theirs. Even I as a small boy could not believe that you had so much water that the rivers were allowed to waste themselves in the sea. All this land needs to make it fertile is water, but alas! there is none. Are we going well for time?'

Biggles looked at his instruments and in the reflector snatched a glance in the direction of the sun now falling towards the horizon behind them. 'We should arrive, as arranged, just before sunset, if my compass has told the truth. From this altitude we should see the oasis.' Biggles smiled. 'I hope it is there. It isn't marked on my map.'

'It is too small, perhaps. You need have no fear of it not being there. To the Arab, an oasis, however small, is a thing to be remembered. It may mean life.'

The aircraft droned on, Biggles' ears, attuned, instinctively listening for any change in the note of the engine. On arrival there would be plenty of room to land, Miktel had assured him. Actually, Biggles was more afraid of not being able to get off, should he find himself on soft sand.

His calculations were proved correct when, as the great orb of the sun touched the western horizon, Miktel exclaimed: 'In front I see the three hills of the Jebel Goz, of which I told you. El Kafala lies beyond. The oasis a little to the left.'

Biggles altered course a trifle and presently, in the mysterious purple twilight, the oasis as conspicuous as an islet in an ocean of water, came into view. He throttled back and began a long glide towards it, eyes questing the inhospitable terrain for any sign of life. But nothing moved.

Neither he nor his companion spoke as, reaching the little group of sun-scorched palms, he made a low circuit and landed, more than a little relieved when the wheels trundled over firm *sabkha*. He taxied on with confidence, knowing that anyone there would have run out to look at them. Finding an opening between the palms he went on into it, turning the nose of the machine to face the open desert should swift departure be necessary. This done he switched off and they got down, Biggles in khaki tropical kit, Miktel in the garments and head-dress of his people. ·

'Well, here we are,' said Biggles. 'Now it's up to you. I hate the idea of you going alone, but if I came I'm afraid I'd do more harm than good.'

'Certainly you would. It is unlikely that the people would harm you, but the Sheikh would soon hear of your arrival and that would defeat our object.'

'Are you sure you'll be all right?'

'Only God is the knower,' returned Miktel, with Moslem piety. 'What is written is written.'

'Well, good luck.'

'What happens will be the will of God,' asserted the lad, with Arab fatalism, and with that he strode away into the gloom.

Biggles watched him go until he was out of sight. Then, from petrol cans that occupied the rear seats, he topped up his tanks as far as the spirit would go, afterwards putting the empty cans in a little depression and covering them with sand. After that, with nothing more to do, he found a seat on a fallen palm and gazed out across the trackless desert. A solemn silence fell.

Time passed, the brooding silence persisting. The moon, huge and pale gold in colour, crept over the horizon to cast weird shadows and people the waste with strange, mystical influences.

An hour passed. Two hours. Three hours, and still the desert lay silent under a moon now clear silver as it rode high in the heavens to dim the faces of a million stars. Midnight came and vanished into the past, with the air cooling rapidly as the arid earth gave up its heat. Biggles began to think the strange thoughts which the Arabs assert come to men who sit too long alone in the wilderness. Uneasiness crept upon him, not so much for himself as for the lad who had so casually walked into what could only be a position of great danger. Should he be found, and his purpose suspected, his fate at the hands of the usurping uncle was a foregone conclusion.

Just what the boy intended to do Biggles did not know, for he had not questioned him as to details. Miktel had merely said that he would find Jerid and bring him back, as if the project presented no great difficulties.

Biggles lit a cigarette, shielding the flame of the match and holding the glowing end of the cigarette within his palm, knowing that in such conditions a single spark would be conspicuous from a long way off.

His watch told him it was three o'clock, still with no sign of Miktel, when, somewhere out in the desert a pebble clicked against another, telling him without a shadow of doubt that someone, or something, was moving. Had the sound come from the right direction he would have supposed it to be Miktel, returning; but it came not from the direction of El Kafala; rather the other way.

Biggles waited. Presently his eyes, probing the darkness, made out, not a jackal as he had hoped, but a compact band of horsemen, coming straight towards him.

He did not move, knowing that if he did he would certainly be seen. There was still a chance that the riders might pass by. But no. They came straight to the oasis, reining their horses to their haunches when they saw the aircraft. Dismounting and unslinging their rifles they walked on slowly without a sound. When they saw Biggles sitting there they stopped.

Biggles had already decided to take the initiative. '*Salaam Aleikum*' (peace be unto you), he said calmly, knowing a few words of Arabic.

'*Aleikum salaam*' (and upon you peace), came the automatic reply.

There was silence that must have lasted a full minute, followed by a low mutter of conversation. Biggles could feel their eyes on him as they strove to grasp a situation that must have had them completely baffled.

Then a man who had been looking at the machine, and may have learned to recognize English letters on the aerodrome at Kuwait, said, accusingly: '*Englesi.*'

'*Bissahi*' (that is true), acknowledged Biggles. 'What men are you that travel by night?'

'We ride in *ghrazzu*,' was the frank reply.

'So that was it,' thought Biggles. The men were raiders.

A voice, speaking in halting guttural English inquired: 'Why does the *ferangi* (foreigner) sit alone in this place?'

Biggles was thinking fast. It seemed reasonable to suppose that if these men were out on a raid they were most likely going to El Kafala. 'I am in the face of Sheikh Jerid Beni Menzil, who is at El Kafala and for whom I wait,' he said, hoping that the men would observe the unwritten law of the desert not to harm the guest of a sheikh.

'*W'Ellah*,' swore the man. 'That is a lie, for as all men know, he is not here.'

'He is at El Kafala, where he is held prisoner by his

uncle who would be sheikh,' insisted Biggles, taking
a chance that the men were of another tribe; or in any
case would not be supporters of the false Sheikh.

This statement was followed by another whispered
conversation. At the end of it, to Biggles' relief, the
riders remounted, and without another word disappeared in the direction of El Kafala with no more
noise than fish swimming away into deep dark water.

It need hardly be said that Biggles found the incident disturbing. Whatever the raiders did was almost
certain to interfere with the rescue plan. This raiding
by different tribes of each other's camels and horses
was more of a sport than actual warfare, as he knew;
but an alarm could not fail to bring the desert to life.
He decided there was nothing he could do about it.
To leave the oasis might be fatal should Miktel arrive
hard pressed. He wondered anxiously just what the
raiders intended to do.

He was soon to know.

He sprang to his feet as the silence was broken by a
distant rifle shot. More followed. Then shouts came
eerily across the barren plain. Yet all he could do was
stand still, watching, waiting, prepared for anything,
irritated by the bad luck that they should have chosen
this particular night for the sortie. He could only hope
that Miktel had got clear of the village before the
raiders struck. There was this about it: the lad would
have warning of the impending attack, for in desert
tribal warfare it is held to be cowardly to strike at men
who might be sleeping.

Minutes passed. Silence had again descended on the
wilderness. There was still nothing Biggles could do.
Had it been daylight he would have taken off and

reconnoitred from the air, but in the darkness he was helpless.

Again the silence was broken, now by the drumming of hooves of horses ridden at full gallop. Four men and some loose horses raced past the oasis without stopping. Sporadic shooting came from several directions. Then more galloping horses, coming towards the oasis. Peering, he could make out two horsemen, riding like furies. Their silhouettes hardened as they drew nearer, making straight for the oasis. Behind them a blurred mass of more riders was materializing in the gloom.

Into the palms dashed the two leading horsemen, to come to a skidding stop in a cloud of dust. A shrill voice, Miktel's voice, shouted: 'Away! Away! We are pursued!'

Biggles jumped to the aircraft. That was all he wanted to know. Shouting 'Get in,' he sprang into the cockpit. As the engine came to life the oasis was filled suddenly with men, horses and noise. But the Proctor was now moving, its airscrew kicking up clouds of dust. For a few moments of confusion it seemed that collision was inevitable. Then the machine was clear, streaking tail-up across the *sabkha*.

Not until he had grabbed some altitude did Biggles call: 'Did you get Jerid?'

'Yes. He is here,' answered Miktel.

'Good work,' complimented Biggles.

Later, on a course for Kuwait, where Biggles intended to refuel, Miktel explained. It seemed that the raid had helped him. He had found Jerid in the *mukhaad* (the men's quarters) and they were on their way out of the village together when the escape was discovered. They would certainly have been overtaken had not raiders announced their arrival by shouting at the horse guards. In the pandemonium that followed no one took any notice of them although they were in some danger of being hit by bullets in the indiscriminate shooting. However, they had managed to seize two horses.

'Then we came away quickly,' stated Miktel simply.

Biggles smiled. 'I'll bet you did.'

'Some men of the village took us for raiders stealing their horses, I think, and pursued us; but with less weight on their backs our horses were faster,' said Miktel, casually, as if the occurrence was an everyday affair. 'It was as God willed,' he concluded.

'Without a doubt,' agreed Biggles.

The Proctor droned on across the wilderness with the false dawn announcing the approach of another day.

At Kuwait they waited for the reserve machine to join them, which it did, flown by Ginger, later in the day. Travelling by easy stages they all arrived home a week later. Jerid then sent word to El Kafala that he was returning home to take up his rightful position, which he did, with an escort of R.A.F. machines, arriving amid scenes of enthusiasm; for seeing which way the wind was blowing his uncle had fled.

That is why, today, Jerid is Sheikh, and Miktel is his court physician.

4

ROUTINE PATROL

SWINGING his flying cap Air Constable 'Ginger' Hebble-thwaite strolled into his operations headquarters to find his colleagues busy on the ever-mounting files of world-wide Aviation news.

Biggles only half glanced up, for Ginger had merely been on one of the regular Air Police coast patrols, on this occasion covering a section of the Highlands of Scotland – out by the east coast and home over the west. Possibly because these patrols rarely yielded anything of interest there was a tendency to treat them with indifference.

'Anything doing?' asked Biggles, casually.

'I'm not sure,' answered Ginger slowly, dropping into a chair. 'I might say no. But following your rule that anything unusual should be followed up, then I must say yes.'

'Go ahead,' requested Biggles. 'We're listening.'

'After turning for home, flying at five thousand, I struck a patch of mist. I reckoned I was running down the west coast, but there must have been more drift than I knew and I was over the sea. I only realized this when I hit the clear and saw the drink, and an island, a small-ish place that seemed to rise sheer out of the water.'

'One of the Western Isles,' murmured Biggles. 'There are plenty of them.'

'I don't know its name but I should recognize it if I saw it again,' continued Ginger. 'As I looked down on it I saw a smudge of smoke. Someone had a fire going, although if ever a lump of land looked uninhabited, that one did. Thinking of castaways I went downhill to investigate, whereupon the fire was doused as if someone had chucked a bucket of water on it. I had a feeling that someone who didn't want to be seen had suddenly spotted me, or heard me. Anyway, castaways were a bad guess. There would surely have been more smoke had that been the answer.'

'You're sure this smoke wasn't a low patch of fog?'

'Quite sure. It came up like chimney smoke. The rest of the island was in the clear.'

'What did you do?'

'I circled and quartered the island several times. Then, seeing nothing, I went on my way.'

'Could it have been one of these bird-watcher chappies on the job?' offered Bertie.

'Why should a bird-watcher take cover, and what was he doing with a fire, anyway?' said Biggles. 'Did you look for a boat, Ginger?'

'Of course. There wasn't one. In fact, I couldn't see a beach. But there was certainly a fire, and fires don't light themselves on rocks or wet moss.'

'Sounds a bit odd,' conceded Biggles.

'Could the smoke have been a signal to someone on the mainland?' suggested Algy. 'How far were you from it?'

'Only about a mile or so; but that isn't the answer. What's the sense of lighting a smoke signal in a fog?'

'And why douse a signal when there was a chance of it being observed, which according to Ginger is what happened?' said Biggles. 'I don't like leaving puzzles unsolved so it might be a good thing to have another look at the place. Let's assume there *is* someone there. As the weather is anything but warm he would light a fire even if he didn't need one for cooking. If the chap needed a fire by day he'd need one still more at night. It should be easy to spot it in the dark. You pin-pointed the position of this little mystery, Ginger?'

'Yes.'

'Then I suggest you go back tonight for another dekko, taking Bertie with you for a double check. Make your approach at ten thousand, cut your engine and glide over in case our unknown friend has another bucket of water handy to put the fire out.'

'Wouldn't it be easier to land and settle the matter?' asked Algy.

'When you've seen this lump of rock you'll think twice about putting an aircraft down on it,' declared Ginger, grimly. 'Come with us and have a look.'

'Let's leave it at that,' decided Biggles, resuming his work.

He was still at it at midnight, with coffee beside him, when the reconnaissance party returned.

'He's there all right,' asserted Algy. 'Had a fire going where it could only be seen from topsides.'

'You're getting me really curious,' averred Biggles. 'It might be a smuggling racket. It's time we had a closer look.'

'The only aircraft that could make a landing on the island would be a helicopter,' stated Algy. 'I doubt if you could get ashore in a boat except in a dead calm sea.'

'How is the sea?'

'Rough.'

'Which means that whoever is on the island will be stuck there until the sea goes down,' said Biggles. 'In the morning I'll get the chief to organize the loan of a service helicopter. It might also be a good thing for us to refresh our memories from the Yard's list of missing persons. Now I'm for bed.'

Two days later, a little before noon, a helicopter buzzed its way northward over the long string of lonely isles that rampart Scotland's west coast against the eternal battering of the Atlantic.

'That's the one,' Ginger told Biggles, who was at the controls. He pointed to a forbidding mass of rock perhaps half a mile long and less than half that distance wide. The only conspicuous feature was a deep corrie that gave the island the appearance of having been struck by a giant axe.

'It's hard to believe that anyone could be there from choice,' remarked Biggles, as he went in and landed on the only spot possible, a shallow depression filled with shale and a few wind-torn tufts of heather. Screaming gulls were the only hazard; but the landing was made without collision and anchors fore and aft adjusted to hold the machine secure in a stiffish breeze.

'Where was the fire?' asked Biggles.

'It isn't easy to say from ground level, but it was roughly about the middle,' answered Ginger.

The search started, and was continued without result until past midday, when a break was made for

food. It was then resumed, again to no purpose. Of a
human being there was no trace. Late in the afternoon,
after a glance at his watch and the sky, Biggles
announced his intention of leaving. 'If there *is* anyone
here he's taking good care no one finds him,' he said,
sceptically.

Ginger spoke positively. 'You doubt it? I'm as sure
as I stand here that there's someone on this crag –
unless the island's kidding itself it's a volcano.'

'Then go ahead and find him.'

'Okay. You push off and leave me here,' said Ginger,
with a touch of asperity. 'You can come back for me
in the morning. When this smart Alec sees you go
he'll come out of his hole thinking he's got away with
it.'

'You'll find it chilly.'

'All the more reason for me to find the fire,' said
Ginger crisply. 'This is my pigeon and I'll see it
through.'

'Fair enough, if that's how you want it,' agreed
Biggles. 'I'll be back soon after daybreak. Come on,
chaps, let's go.'

Ginger sat on a rock and watched the helicopter de-
part, and with its departure some of his confidence
departed, too, for a more bleak, inhospitable place
would have been hard to imagine. The sun dipped
into the Atlantic, and with the coming of darkness
the temperature dropped sharply, so to seek shelter
from the wind he made his way to the corrie and
descending a little way took up a position in some deep
heather.

Within a few minutes he saw the fire – not the actual
fire but the flickering glow of it on the opposite side

of the corrie. Rising, he made a somewhat dangerous descent to the bottom and then along a trickle of water to the objective. Presently, against the light, he made out a vague silhouette – a man in a kilt, he took it to be, squatting on a stone at the mouth of a cave. Only at the last moment was he seen, and his astonishment was great when a female voice with a Scots brogue said: 'Come one step nearer and I shoot!'

Ginger stopped. 'Take it easy,' he requested. 'The plane will be back tomorrow and if I'm not here to meet it the place will be combed until you're found; so shooting me won't help you. Mind if I come closer? It's chilly outside.' So saying he advanced, noting that the woman was in fact holding a revolver. He judged her to be in the early twenties, and good-looking in a wild sort of way. Finding a seat he said: 'Are you doing this for a bet or something?'

The reply was a question. 'Who are you?'

'I'm a flying policeman,' answered Ginger. 'Seeing your fire from upstairs I thought I'd spotted a cast-away – or hit on a smuggling racket. What are you doing here?'

The girl hesitated. 'I'm hiding.'

'From whom?'

'People like you.'

'How long have you been here?'

'Three months.'

'Suffering seagulls! What do you use for food?'

'I manage.'

'Why do the police want you?'

'I shot a man.'

Ginger looked hard at the face in the firelight. He was of course acquainted with the descriptions of people missing or wanted. He thought he recognized her. 'Are you by any chance Margaret Laretski?'

'Aye. I am that.'

'You shot your husband – a Pole. Why did you do it?'

'He was a devil as well as a crook. I stuck it till he killed my child in one of his fits of temper. He would have killed me too, at the end, so I shot him with his own gun and bolted here.'

'Why here?'

'I come from just across the water. I have clansmen there. One, who wanted to marry me before I was fool enough to marry that Pole, brings me food when the weather's right. We were going to keep it up till the murder was forgotten, when we were going to Australia.'

'What murder?'

'My husband.'

'But you didn't kill him. You only knocked him out, and enabled the police to find a man they'd been looking for for years, for the murder of his first wife. He was tried, convicted and hanged under his real name. The one he gave you was an alias. That must be why you didn't know about it. All the police wanted you for was evidence, so I don't think you've much to worry about. What have you got in that frying pan?'

'Herring.'

'Then get on with the cooking. This breeze gives one an appetite.'

5

THE LADY FROM BRAZIL

AIR DETECTIVE-INSPECTOR BIGGLESWORTH, walking down the corridor towards his chief's office in Scotland Yard, gave a second glance at a man who was just leaving.

'What's on *his* mind?' he asked, as he entered the office.

Air Commodore Raymond looked up from his desk. 'Who?'

'Wasn't that Foster, of Customs and Excise?'

'It was.'

'He did not, I imagine, call to ask if we were happy?'

'No. He has a problem.'

'And wants us to solve it.'

'That's what we're here for. Sit down and I'll tell you about it. Foster is up against one of those riddles that look simple but are a bit tricky. There lives in Brazil, in Rio de Janeiro to be precise, a handsome young lady named Dolores Cantani. She is a cabaret dancer in a well-known night club. One of her several friends is a man named José da Silvaro, who derives a considerable income from emerald mines somewhere in the interior. He has a brother in London who looks after the European side of the business. Foster has been some time getting these facts lined up, both over here and through our contacts in Rio.'

'The lady has, I presume, visited our happy land.'

'She's making a habit of it,' returned the Air Commodore, dryly. 'The first time she came here Foster paid no particular attention, there being no reason why he should. She came – so she said – for a holiday, arriving at London Airport in an aircraft of Inter-Atlan Airways, which, as you know, is an international concern. She had with her, as presents for her friends, a small parcel of inferior emeralds. She declared them and paid duty.'

'Fair enough.'

'As you say, fair enough. At this time, you understand, Foster knew nothing about her, nothing about da Silvaro or his brother over here. She stayed a week. It was when Foster was making up his returns that it struck him as a bit odd that a dancer should spend several months' pay on an air fare to come here for a week. When, three months later, she turned up again, this time with a few mediocre uncut diamonds, he began to think seriously.'

'Did she declare them?'

'Oh, yes. She paid the duty without a murmur, which was in itself suspicious, because the stones were so small that had she not declared them she could probably have got them through Customs without them being found. She may not have known that one of the most common tricks of non-professional smugglers is to make a great show of honesty by declaring some trivial object in the hope of getting away with something more expensive in the bottom of the bag. Foster, now suspicious, had her searched. He found nothing.

Dolores stayed ten days, having had another expensive holiday for a return fare running into three figures. It was at this time that Foster made inquiries, with results I have told you.'

A slow smile spread over Biggles' face. 'Don't say she came again!'

'She did, about six months ago, bringing her usual flashing smile and a few presents on which, as before, she paid duty without a whimper. This time Foster went as far as he dare. As you know, these fellows develop a sort of instinct where crooks are concerned, and they are seldom wrong. He *knew* she was cheating; yet in spite of all the female searchers could do they found nothing – and they're experts. They know where to look. Dolores, instead of being angry, was slightly amused. Foster was not amused. He had to apologize, and pay compensation for a certain amount of damage done to her luggage. He is prepared to swear she hadn't a single dutiable article on her. He's also prepared to swear, although he hasn't a shred of evidence, that she's working a smuggling racket. After all, trans-atlantic trips are expensive. How could she afford them?'

'Maybe her gem-king boy friend paid the bill.'

'No doubt he did. Boy friends often give presents to their girl friends. But why trips to Europe? What pleasure could da Silvaro get out of that?'

'Having no girl friends I wouldn't know. What does all this add up to?'

'Foster has had the starry-eyed Dolores checked in Rio. She has just bought another return ticket to London. She leaves next Saturday. That gives you a week.'

'A week for what?'

'To get out there and travel back with her. Keep an eye on her. Spot what she's doing, and how she's doing it. She may have a confederate on the plane. If so, signals will pass between them. Something may happen when the plane calls at the Azores for fuel. I don't know. It's up to you.'

Biggles stubbed his cigarette. 'This isn't really in my line but I'll see what I can make of it.'

'All right. I'll radio our agent in Rio to book you a seat on the plane as close as possible to number seven.'

'Why seven?'

'That's the number of her seat. She always has the same one.'

'Why?'

The Air Commodore smiled. 'Ask her. Superstition, perhaps. Seven is a popular number with many people. She says it's the most comfortable seat – least vibration, least noise.'

Biggles nodded. 'She may be right. We'll see.'

When, on the following Saturday, the Inter-Atlan Douglas left Rio for London, Biggles was sitting a few seats behind the good-looking, expensively-dressed brunette who had been pointed out to him as Dolores Cantani. He had watched her in the waiting lounge. He had watched her, and ten other passengers, board the plane without any sign of recognition. This he expected, for he had checked the bona fides of the passengers and found them in order. Of the ten, six were British. All were in legitimate business. The behaviour of Dolores Cantani was in perfect accord with her avowed purpose. She was going to Europe for a holiday.

She took the meals served by the air hostess with the healthy appetite of one without a care in the world. Between meals she read a book, twice ringing for a drink. From time to time she chewed gum, a habit not uncommon in aircraft. Nothing happened at the Azores, and the plane was now on the last leg of its journey to London.

Biggles was puzzled. He was also a little annoyed, for it began to look as if he had made a fruitless journey. A feeling grew on him that on this occasion Foster had been wrong. If previous searches had failed to reveal anything the same was likely to happen again. If the girl was running contraband her method was certainly original.

It was on these lines that Biggles was thinking when the big machine touched down on its runway at London Airport. Here, within the next few minutes, if the girl was in fact guilty, would be his last chance of catching her, for after the passengers had disembarked Foster would take over, as had been arranged.

As the passengers filed away for passport and customs formalities Foster hurried up to him. 'See anything?' queried the Customs officer tersely.

'Nothing,' returned Biggles. 'She didn't speak to anyone. She didn't move from her seat. If she's carrying contraband you'll have to find it. I haven't a clue. I'll wait here,' he concluded, as Foster strode away, tight-lipped.

He watched the pilots and crew pack up and walk away, their work finished. Maintenance men arrived casually, to deal with the aircraft. With them came a plain, dark-eyed girl carrying the equipment to spray the interior of the machine with insecticide and so prevent the importation of malignant mosquitoes or other objectionable insects. A slight frown lined Biggles' forehead as he watched her go to the open door. Her jaws moved in the manner of one chewing gum. Dolores had chewed gum. Was it coincidence or was there more to it?

He walked quickly to the door, and moving quietly, looked inside. The girl was stooping over the seat numbered seven.

As he stepped out Foster returned. 'She's beaten us again,' he muttered. 'A few small emeralds which she declared. It doesn't make sense. Why send someone to London with a parcel which, as the contents were declared, might as well have been sent by post?'

'A girl is disinfecting the plane – a dark-eyed lass with black hair,' replied Biggles evenly. 'Do you know her?'

'Sounds like Miss Varros. That's her job. What about it?'

'Let's see how well she does it,' suggested Biggles, moving forward.

Foster stared. 'What's the idea?'

'She chews gum. It can be useful stuff. There was a time when most long-distance pilots carried it to plug a possible leaky tank.'

The girl came down the steps just as they reached them. Biggles stopped her. 'Excuse me, are you Miss Varros?'

The girl moved something in her mouth before she answered. 'Yes.'

'You like chewing gum?'

D

Some of the colour left the girl's face. 'What about it?'

'I'm wondering if it's the same brand that Miss Cantani uses. May we see it?'

Any colour that was left drained from the face of the spray-gun operator.

'Be careful not to swallow it,' warned Biggles. 'The consequences might be serious.'

For perhaps five seconds the girl stared at Biggles stonily. Then she ejected something into her hand and passed to Biggles what looked like a lump of clay. 'Okay,' she said quietly. 'I see you know. I told her she'd do it once too often.'

Biggles opened the gum to expose two magnificent emeralds. He handed them to Foster. 'Is this what you've been looking for?'

Said Foster, looking at the girl, 'Why did you do it?'

'Dolores is my half sister,' was the answer. 'She and Mr da Silvaro, for whom I used to work, and who helped me to get this job, persuaded me into it. It looked easy, I must say.'

Said Biggles: 'She stuck the stones under seat seven with chewing gum; you collected them and handed them to her later.'

'To da Silvaro,' returned the girl bitterly. 'He wasn't taking chances.'

'I'll see you inside, Miss Varros,' said Foster curtly. As the girl walked away he turned to Biggles. 'Thanks,' he said. 'If ever you're out of a job come and see me.'

Smiling, Biggles took a cigarette from his case. 'Not for me,' he murmured. 'Being flown by people I don't know frightens me to death. You can buy me a drink, instead.'

6

EQUATORIAL
ENCOUNTER

BIGGLES was in the Air Police office discussing some
recently released aircraft performance figures with his
police pilots when the intercom. telephone buzzed.

'That will be the Old Man,' he said, as he reached
for the receiver. 'I know his buzz. Hello, sir,' he went
on, speaking into the instrument. He listened for a
moment. 'Okay, sir. I'll be down right away.' He
glanced at the others as he got up. 'Wants to see me,'
he explained. 'From his tone of voice I'd say he has
something urgent on his mind so stand by to pull on
your seven-league boots.'

He went down to the office of the chief of his depart-
ment, Air Commodore Raymond, of the Special Air
Police, knocked, and without waiting for a reply,
entered.

The Air Commodore was at his desk with some
papers in front of him. 'Come in,' he requested. 'Sit
down. We may be some time. Have a cigarette.' He
pushed the box forward.

'Thank you, sir,' accepted Biggles. 'What's the hurry
this time?'

'It's a longish story. I'd better run over the whole thing so that you can get all the angles from the outset.'

Biggles lit his cigarette.

'Some years ago,' stated the Air Commodore, 'a certain foreign motor tyre manufacturer thought he could produce rubber more cheaply than he could buy it from us in Malaya; so he took some land in the country from which rubber first came, Brazil, and planted his own trees. You may remember what happened.'

'He planted them too close together, with the result they were attacked by a disease and died.'

'Right. Not to be thwarted he cleared more jungle in Liberia, the Negro state on the coast of West Africa, and tried again. More trees were planted, but it seemed that the people there didn't care much for manual labour, so as it is no place for a white man to work with his hands, again the scheme looked like being a failure. However, later on, as the trees matured and the price of rubber went up, some people did muster the energy to tap the trees, and a fair amount of rubber is now exported. Others did even better. Following the example of a Scot named Anderson they planted certain other trees that yield valuable gums and essential oils now in demand by modern industry. These products came to the coast, to Monrovia, the capital, where they were picked up as extra cargo by passing ships. We came to rely on this source of these particular commodities. You follow me?'

'Perfectly.'

'A short while ago these supplies, for no apparent reason, began to dwindle. They became less and less and have now fizzled out altogether, greatly to the concern of the people who depended on them.'

'Bad luck.'

'Maybe luck had nothing to do with it. It's a serious matter. Where is the stuff going?'

'Can't this chap Anderson tell you?'

'We've lost touch with him.'

'Perhaps there isn't any more stuff. The natives could have got tired again.'

'That isn't the answer. We infiltrated an agent. He couldn't find Anderson, but he reports that work is still going on, if anything harder than ever. I repeat, where is the stuff going? The shortage is putting us to quite a lot of inconvenience and holding up certain exports.'

'Obviously, it's going out another way – through Sierra Leone, Ghana, the Ivory Coast or Guinea. What does this agent fellow think about it?'

'He's a coloured man, a Jamaican named Joseph Nelson. For a time we had messages regularly. The last one said there were rumours of aircraft operating to and from the hinterland, using a new airstrip, and he was trying to confirm it. That was a month ago. Since when we've heard nothing.'

'You think he went a bit too far and ran into trouble?'

'It begins to look like that. Nelson was a thoroughly reliable man.'

'I don't quite see what the excitement is about. Surely if Anderson, or the locals, have found a better market, it's up to them to take it.'

'Agreed, provided pressure is not being used to force them, against their wishes, to do that. Are they

getting more money? We don't know. What is certain
is this: we are now being compelled to buy these commodities in another market, and pay through the
nose for them. There is a suspicion that we are actually getting the same stuff through different channels –
at double the price.'

'In other words, a middleman has stepped in and
is skimming the cream off the milk.'

'Yes. He may be working for himself or for an
organization in competition with us. If the raw
material goes up in price it follows that the finished
product must go up too, with the result that our com-
petitors can undercut us and we lose the orders. But
as I say, this is fair enough provided the natives are
getting a square deal; but if they have been turned into
a sort of labour force, with the deliberate intention
of working against our interests, it becomes a different
matter altogether.'

'If the profits are high enough, air transport, even
in those conditions, would become a proposition,' murmured Biggles. 'With plenty of labour available the
clearing of an area for a landing ground would present
no great difficulty. Did this chap Nelson give you any
idea of the position of this alleged airstrip?'

'No. Obviously he didn't know or he'd have reported
it. He was, presumably, on his way to confirm the
rumour when he sent in his last message.'

'Where was he then?'

'He said he was somewhere near the frontiers of
Liberia and French territory.'

'That's a bit vague.'

'It couldn't be otherwise. There are no actual boundaries.'

'He was evidently well inland.'

'Yes. But there is this about it. The place from which
Nelson wrote, which must have been no great distance
from the airstrip – assuming that there is one – would
be within easy flying distance of Sierra Leone, or the
Ivory Coast, either of which could be used for re-
fuelling and maintenance. No doubt your friend,
Marcel Brissac of the Paris Sûreté, would arrange
facilities for you at French airfields should it be
necessary.'

'I see.' Biggles stubbed his cigarette. 'I take it you'd
like me to run out there and cast an eye over the
district for you.'

'We must do that if for no other purpose than to
find out what has become of Anderson and Nelson.'

'Haven't we any people on the ground there who
could do that?'

'Possibly. But I'm thinking of the time factor. Over-
land travel in that part of the world can't be anything
but slow. The only thing that travels fast is news, which
means that if there's any funny business going on the
people responsible would hear of the approach of an
investigating officer long before he got there, and take
steps accordingly. If, as it seems, we're dealing with
aviation, it would be better, anyway, to have an air
expert on the job.'

Biggles nodded. 'All right, sir. I don't like these
frontier assignments because you never know whose
toes you're treading on; but I'll go out and see what I
can make of it.'

'Be careful. It's a bit tricky. Don't upset Liberia.
They're likely to be very touchy.'

'There you go,' said Biggles sadly. 'Raising snags

before I start. But don't worry. I shall probably park myself at Freetown, in Sierra Leone, and operate from there. Alternatively, if that isn't suitable, I could arrange to use Kankan, in Guinea. Anyway, I'll find a base somewhere and make a general survey for this landing strip, or any other signs of aviation. If there is dirty work going on it's pretty certain there will be a white man in the background, in which case he'll have a headquarters. When I find it you can tell me what do next.'

The Air Commodore smiled. 'Fair enough.'

'Well, I'll get on with it,' concluded Biggles.

From his base at Freetown, Sierra Leone, using the Air Police Wellington with its full crew, for nearly a week Biggles had searched the northern frontiers of Liberia without result. This meant flying over French territory, but satisfied in his mind that nothing could pass through the British colonies on either side without being observed, with the consent of Interpol Headquarters in Paris he had concentrated on the north. Marcel Brissac, of the Sûreté, knew what he was doing, but having no particular interest in the assignment had not joined him.

The nature of the country below, upon which he had often looked down, was not, on the face of it, the sort to simplify his task, consisting as it did for the most part of equatorial rain forest, sometimes flat and sometimes mountainous, that gave way only in certain areas to scrub and sandy wastes. Farther north, towards Senegal, this in turn broke down to true desert.

Yet from the very fact that the country was so heavily wooded he felt sure that an open space large enough for an aircraft landing should not be difficult to find – if, in fact, one was there. As he said, there was a doubt about it, for the only evidence of its existence was through unsubstantiated native rumour. The doubt became larger as time went on, due to some extent perhaps to the constant anxiety of wondering where he himself would get down in the event of engine trouble, particularly when in the region of the formidable Nimba mountains.

However, on the morning of the sixth day the matter was brought to a head in a way that not only settled the issue but explained why the quest had so far been unsuccessful.

They were over scrub country when Ginger, who was sitting beside him, suddenly exclaimed: 'Bandit below us under the port bow.'

Biggles' eyes switched to the direction indicated.

An aircraft, flying over two thousand feet below their own altitude of four thousand, appeared to be gliding over the tree-tops like a giant dragonfly.

Even as he spotted it his hand was pushing the throttle wide open for power to climb between the stranger and the sun, a position from which he hoped, if he had not already been seen, to escape observation. 'It's coming from the east,' he remarked. 'What do you make of it?'

'Looks like one of those twin-engined Samsons the Americans were mass-producing at the end of the war for freight hauling.'

'I think you're right,' agreed Biggles, throttling back to cruising speed and turning slowly to follow. 'I'd rather not get any closer at the moment. Tell the others we have struck the trail.'

Ginger passed the news on the intercom. 'If that chap's flying a compass course, and is dead on it, I don't know where he's making for,' he said, studying the map on his knees. 'There's no possible objective straight in front of him – just wild country. And if he goes much farther he'll be over the big timber.'

'Take a look at the carpet and you'll see where he's making for,' returned Biggles dryly.

Staring down Ginger saw the astonishing spectacle of shrubs and bushes moving aside to leave an open area between them. 'Well, knock me for six,' he ejaculated.

'Honest men in peace-time don't need to camouflage their airfields,' observed Biggles cynically. 'Whatever their game is they're up to no good. No wonder we couldn't find the airstrip! There he goes down. I'll move away a bit so that they don't hear our engine noise when they switch off.'

'They may have seen us already.'

'We can take no harm by supposing they haven't. We're in the sun, and the people down there will naturally be watching their own machine.'

For another five minutes Biggles held his course away from the landing ground. Then he started slowly to turn again. 'Could you pin-point that strip?' he asked.

'To within a mile or two, if you call that a pin-point. There's nothing I can see to mark the frontier.'

'Do you reckon it to be in French territory or Liberia?'

'I'd say just over the French side.'

'We can argue it later,' asserted Biggles. 'I'm going to land there to see what goes on.'

'Isn't that taking a chance?'

'Perhaps. But we shall have to land there some time and I can't see any advantage to be gained by delay. Moreover, it might not be easy to find the place again when they've replaced the shrubbery. They're not actually obstructions. From the way they were being carried they're too flimsy for that. All the same, we should look silly if we tried to get down in the wrong place and ran into something solid. I see they've got the machine out of sight already. A nice little set-up.'

As the Wellington glided on Biggles announced his plan to the others. 'When we get on the floor I shall take Ginger with me and have a look round. I want you, Algy and Bertie, to remain in the machine, in the cockpit, ready for a snappy take-off should it become necessary. It might be as well if you kept your heads down so that the people below won't know there's anyone else on board. Okay?'

'Okay,' confirmed Algy.

Looking ahead as Biggles made his approach Ginger could see some men standing on the fringe of the shade cast by trees that straggled forward from the forest. They were close together, faces upturned, apparently in conversation as they watched the Wellington touch down and run to a stop near them. Their aircraft stood farther back under the same trees.

Leaving the Wellington with its nose pointing to open ground Biggles switched off and jumped down. Ginger followed, his eyes busy. He noted several palm-thatched huts far enough back under the trees to prevent them from being seen from above.

With Biggles he walked towards the men who, with expressionless faces, stood watching them. Two were definitely white men. There was a doubt about two others. Near-by a filthy Negro squatted on the ground gnawing a bone. From his fantastic dress he was clearly a witch-doctor, or perhaps some sort of chief.

'Good morning,' greeted Biggles, speaking in English, that being the standard language used in Liberia.

'Lost your way?' queried one of the men. He spoke with a strong American accent.

'Not exactly,' returned Biggles. 'We happened to spot your airstrip, and not being able to find it on our map we dropped in to make sure we were not fooling ourselves. What are you doing here?'

'Surveying for a new air route. What do you reckon you're doing? You've been up and down a good many times lately. We've seen you. Where have you come from?'

'Freetown,' answered Biggles. 'We, too, have been having a look round with a view to opening up the district.' He smiled, indicating the witch-doctor. 'Is this a sample of the passengers you hope to carry?'

The second white man spoke curtly. 'We shall carry freight.' He, too, had an accent, but it gave no indication of his nationality.

'Queer we didn't notice your airstrip before,' said Biggles casually.

'You must fly with your eyes shut. It's always here. We ain't got nothing to hide.'

'I didn't suggest that you had,' replied Biggles, blandly. 'Just as a matter of interest, are we in Liberia or on French colonial soil? The boundaries are not easy to see.'

'I wouldn't know. Does it matter?'

Biggles shrugged. 'It might. It depends on how people feel about their property.'

The man grinned unpleasantly. 'We'll chance it.'

'Okay, if that's how you feel about it,' said Biggles. 'We'll get along.'

At this juncture, by what was a piece of bad luck for the men there, although they appeared not to realize it, there came from no great distance away a series of sounds that brought a frown of perplexity to Biggles' face. One suggested that a small-bore rifle was being fired.

'What's that?' he asked.

The men looked at each other. One muttered something under his breath, and made as if to walk away; but he had only taken a step or two when the cause of the noise appeared from the forest. It was a line of Negroes carrying heavy loads. Beside them marched a white man, carrying, and sometimes cracking, a whip. Reaching one of the sheds the blacks dropped their loads and sank down like men exhausted by a long journey.

'Do you have to do that?' asked Biggles quietly.

'Do what?'

'Use a whip on these fellows.'

'It lets them see who's boss.'

'What's that stuff they've just brought in?'

'Local produce.'

Biggles inclined his head towards the witch-doctor. 'What does he have to say about it?'

The man smiled unpleasantly. 'Oh, him! He organizes it. Keeps the mob in order when they're inclined to kick. Funny business, this mumbo-jumbo stuff, but the poor fools believe in it.'

'So I understand,' murmured Biggles evenly.

'That old bag o' bones has only to tell one of 'em that he's a' goin' to die and the poor guy just sits down and dies. It don't make sense to me, but there it is.'

'As you say, there it is,' agreed Biggles. 'Well, we'll be on our way.'

'I wouldn't say anything about this near the coast – you know how it is.'

'What do you mean by that?'

'Wa'al, you know how some people talk, always ready to start a scream about what they call the ill-treatment of their poor black brothers.'

'Maybe they have reason to.'

'What are you trying to give me?'

'It all depends.'

'On what?'

'Several things.'

'Smart guy, eh. Nobody asked you to poke your nose in. What goes on here is no concern of yours, so forget it.'

Biggles hesitated. 'You may be right, at that,' he agreed.

'Sure I'm right. And if you're wise you'll remember it.'

Biggles did not answer. Turning, he walked back to the Wellington.

'Are you going to let 'em get away with that?' demanded Ginger indignantly, as they climbed in.

'I hope not,' answered Biggles. 'At the moment we're in no position to argue. Before we can do that we shall have to know whose ground we're standing on. If it's French, all right. If it's Liberia we shall have to step warily.'

'What about Anderson? That bunch could tell you what happened to him.'

'If he's still alive another day or two won't hurt him. If he's dead, there's even less need for haste. Those fellows were satisfied in their minds that we were just a couple of mug Britishers; but had we made a move towards those sheds I fancy their behaviour would have been very different. They fell for my bluff that we were merely having a look round. Had they suspected what we were really doing here they'd have shown their teeth -- the teeth I could see bulging from their pockets. The rats. Little they care what mischief they do. Now you see how rumours get about of white men beating up the natives in their colonies. Don't worry. It shouldn't take us long to get this business buttoned up now we know what's going on.'

They climbed into the plane, and Biggles took off.

From a distance, looking back, Ginger could see the bushes being replaced.

'Looks as if we're back to slavery, old boy,' came Bertie's voice over the intercom.

'It won't go on much longer,' promised Biggles. 'We've found what we were looking for. The Air Commodore wasn't far out in his summing up of the situation.'

'What do you reckon is going on?' asked Ginger.

'It's pretty obvious. That nasty piece of work who did the talking must have known about Anderson's produce going through to the coast and decided to grab it for himself. There may be behind him a big businessman who wants the stuff, or sees a way to make easy money by raising the price of it. But that's as may be. We'll deal with the man on the spot. His job wasn't very difficult. All he had to do was get that witch-doctor in his pocket, probably by bribery. The witch-doctor would then give orders to those wretched blacks, who wouldn't dare to disobey. The fellow said that himself.'

'But what about Anderson?'

'We shall find out what happened to him in due course. The gang may have gone to him, and others, with an offer for their produce. Anderson, we may be sure, would refuse to have anything to do with such a deal. If they tried to force him, he, being a Scot, would fight, but even he would be helpless against what that fellow rightly called mumbo-jumbo. Anyway, something like that must have happened, with the result that Anderson has disappeared. Nelson, the agent sent to investigate, must have been hot on the trail when he, too, ran into trouble.'

'Where are you making for now?' asked Ginger.

'Kankan. From there I'll send a cable to Marcel. The next step is to find out on whose territory that airstrip has been laid out. I'm hoping it will turn out to be on French soil, because Marcel could then act with authority, which we could not. If we took the law into our own hands we should find ourselves in the wrong, particularly if a foreign national was hurt.'

'Suppose the place happens to be in Liberia?'

'In that case we shall have to take a chance and handle things our own way, whatever may come of it. Anderson and Nelson may still be alive. We can't abandon them. If they've been murdered – well, even though the roof flies off the House of Commons, or any other parliament building, I'll see that somebody pays for it.'

'The Air Commodore would throw a fit if he heard you talking like that,' said Ginger, smiling.

'He knew when he took me on that in some things I go my own way,' answered Biggles, grimly. 'I'm not standing for murder for him or anyone else.'

Ginger said no more.

The Wellington flew on, and in the early afternoon landed at Kankan, the airport in Guinea. From there Biggles sent a cable to Marcel asking him to join them as quickly as possible, bringing with him the largest scale map available of the district concerned.

They had to wait for three days for his arrival. Then, in the airport waiting-room, with the map Marcel had brought open in front of them, Biggles explained the position. 'That's the spot, as near as I can make it,' he concluded, marking the map with his pencil.

'It's on our soil, but only just,' decided Marcel. 'This may answer a question for me, too. There is now so much increase of freight at Port Bouet, on the Ivory Coast, that the Customs men there complain they are overworked.'

'How does that come into it?'

'A railway links Porte Bouet with Bouflé, in the interior. It is from Bouflé that these goods are coming. There is also at Bouflé an aerodrome. It is to the east of this mark you have made. The plane you saw came from the east. *Voila!* It adds up, as you say, *mon ami*. It could be from Port Bouet that the merchandise carried by these slaves leaves the country.'

'By thunder! I believe you've got it,' declared Biggles. 'The stuff is flown to Bouflé, and there put on rail for the coast where it is picked up and shipped by a contact man working with the gang.'

Marcel shrugged. 'It is so simple. The goods are not contraband. Duty can be paid and all is well. *Tiens – tiens – tiens.*'

'It may be well for you, but not for us.'

'What do you want me to do?'

'Do you allow slavery in your colonies?'

'But of course not.'

'Very well. Here's the answer. This gang, operating on French soil, is forcing natives to work by threats and violence. You must investigate; and while you're doing that we'll do a little investigating, too.'

'Tell me this, old dog,' requested Marcel. 'Why do these men have the dirty necks to work on French ground?'

'For the simple reason there's no other spot within miles from which an aircraft could operate. It would need an army of men to cut an airstrip in the Liberian forest.'

'So,' breathed Marcel. 'Always you have the answer. Let us go. I will ask to see their permission to make an aerodrome on French soil. Let us hope they are rude, and make trouble.'

'Why?'

'Because if they say they are sorry, they make a mistake, what can we do? They retire to Liberia, and wait until we have gone to start again. But if they throw their weights about, *la la*, I put them in prison for resistance to the police.'

Biggles smiled. 'That,' he said softly, 'should put them out of business.'

'*Bon.* We go in the morning. Some of our policemen

shall come with us. But what if the bushes are put out?
How do we land?'

'I can find the place. As for the bushes, if we touch
them they are so light they could do no harm.'

'*Entendu.*'

Early the next morning, the Wellington, with Marcel
and four French colonial policemen, in uniform, in the
cabin, took off and headed for the secret airfield.

As it happened the camouflage had been removed,
the reason being that the Samson was being loaded,
and would soon, presumably, take off for another flight.
The arrival of the Wellington over the scene caused
this work to be suspended, those engaged in it form-
ing a compact little group to watch it land.

Biggles went in, taxied on to where the men and the
machine were standing, and switched off. 'Go ahead,
Marcel,' he said. 'Watch out for trouble. These stiffs
may think that so far from the coast they can get away
with anything. I'm with you.'

Marcel, now in charge of the operation, jumped
down, followed by the rest. He marched up to the
group and addressed the man who had acted as spokes-
man on the occasion of Biggles' previous visit.

'What are you doing here?' he demanded.

'You can see for yourself, can't you? We've nothing
to hide,' was the insolent answer.

'If you've nothing to hide why try to hide it with
camouflage?' Marcel pointed to the heaps of bushes.
Nodding towards a huddle of Negroes he went on:
'Who are these men? What are they doing here.'

'What's that got to do with you?'

'It has plenty to do with me,' returned Marcel

crisply. 'You're on French government property and I want to see your papers.'

The man, pale with anger, glared at Biggles. 'I suppose I can thank you for this, you dirty, sneaking snooper –'

'All right. Cut the compliments,' rasped Biggles. 'Being abusive won't help you.'

'What do you mean?'

'You should know. Your little game is about played out.'

'Who says so?'

'I say so.'

'You and who else?'

'The French police.'

Marcel stepped in. 'That is enough. Where is your permission from my government to make an aerodrome here?'

'What are you trying to give me?' snarled the man. 'I don't need no papers.'

'So you haven't any,' said Marcel coldly. 'In that case you are all under arrest.'

Biggles took a pace nearer to the blacks, many of whom bore marks of the whip. Pointing to the pile of bundles awaiting shipment he asked: 'Does this belong to Mr Anderson?'

There was no answer. The Negroes huddled closer together, eyes rolling, with furtive glances towards the witch-doctor, obviously terrified of him.

Biggles spoke directly to one who looked more intelligent than the rest. 'You savvy Mr Anderson?'

At this stage of the proceedings, the gang, as if they had suddenly realized that Biggles had spoken the truth when he had said the game was up, or were prompted by Biggles' reference to Anderson, went into action. Guns appeared in their hands and they began backing towards the Samson, apparently with the intention of departing in it.

'You stand where you are, all of you, or I'll let daylight into you,' the leader spat vindictively.

Biggles, his main purpose achieved, in the hope of avoiding casualties was prepared to let them go, confident that they could be apprehended later no matter where they went. But one of Marcel's men, acting on his own initiative, bravely but foolishly ran forward to get between them and the machine.

'Get out o' my way,' snarled the leader of the opposition.

The policeman took no notice.

A gun crashed. He stumbled and fell.

Biggles' gun and Marcel's little police automatic cracked together and the man who had fired the shot crumpled.

The others, one of whom must have been the Samson pilot, made a run for the machine. Some shots were fired but no one else was hit.

'Let them go – we'll get them later,' shouted Biggles, anxious to avoid more bloodshed, for which there was now no real justification.

Marcel accepted the advice.

It must have been the pilot who was first into the Samson, for almost at once the metal airscrews flashed as the engines sprang to life.

Why the witch-doctor acted as he did must remain a matter for conjecture. Without the support of the white men he may have feared the vengeance of those of his countrymen for whose miserable plight he had been responsible. He may have thought he would be hanged for his criminal activities. Anyway, the sound of the engines must have told him that he was being abandoned, for springing to his feet, mouthing and screaming, he raced after his late employers. The door was slammed in his face, whereupon, before anything could be done to prevent it, he ran on towards the nose of the machine apparently with some wild hope of preventing it from leaving. He made a fatal mistake, one which has often been made before; and if mechanics can make it, as they have, in an ignorant Negro it was understandable. He ran straight into an airscrew. There was a horrid *snick* as metal struck bone and the man sprawled headlong. He lay still.

'He's had it,' breathed Ginger.

'That's about what he deserved, the dirty old scoundrel,' observed Bertie.

'I reckon it'll take more than witches to doctor him on his feet again,' said Algy, as the Samson's engines bellowed, sending dust and grass swirling as it moved forward.

'It's probably better this way,' observed Biggles, as they watched the machine take off and swing round to the east. 'The next thing is to find out what happened to Anderson and Nelson.'

He walked over to the cowering blacks. 'You savvy Mr Anderson, you men?' he questioned, in a voice likely to gain confidence.

'Yaas, boss,' answered one, tremulously.

'Speak up. You've nothing to be afraid of now. Where is he?'

Nervously the man answered, pointing at a small hut. 'He's over dare, boss. We work for Massa Anderson one time. Him good boss. We don't want go back on him but we has to. We'se scared pretty bad, boss.'

'I know,' answered Biggles, and strode towards the hut indicated. The door was padlocked. 'Break this door down,' he ordered.

A big Negro picked up a log of wood, struck the lock a tremendous blow and the door flew open. Biggles went in, peering in the gloom after the glare outside, for there was no window.

Ginger, who had followed him, made out two figures. One was lying down, half raised on an elbow. The other, a white man in filthy tropical kit, was standing.

Said Biggles, addressing him: 'Are you Mr Anderson?'

'Aye.'

'Are you all right?'

'Nae sa bad. Touch o' fever, that's all.'

'Who's this with you?'

'Lad named Nelson. He's had a rough time. What's happening outside? Did I hear shooting?'

'You did. We're police officers. We dropped in to tidy the place up.'

'It's time somebody dropped in,' quoth the Scot, dourly.

Biggles smiled. 'Ah well. Better late than never. I must see what's happening outside. I'll be back. Ginger, you might take care of Nelson.'

He went out to where Marcel was watching Algy and Bertie bandage the wounded policeman's shoulder with kit from the Wellington's first-aid box. 'How is he?' he asked.

'Not too bad. But he's got a bullet in his shoulder

so the sooner a doctor gets to work on him the better.'

'I'll fly him back to Kankan right away. You'll want to be getting back too, Marcel. How's the fellow we shot?'

'Dead.'

'Oh dear! Any idea who he is?'

'I can tell you,' said a voice. Anderson walked up. 'His name's Griggs, a bad hat who has been up and down the Coast for years causing trouble. Nobody will be sorry to hear he's had what's been coming to him for a long time.'

'As he's been identified you'd better get your fellows to bury him, Marcel,' said Biggles. 'There's no point in taking a corpse home with us but we can't leave him lying here. How about the witch-doctor?'

Algy answered. 'A blade caught him on the skull so he's gone to where it'll take more than mumbo-jumbo to bring him back.'

'All right. As soon as your fellows have finished, Marcel, I'll fly you all back to Kankan. Then I'll go on and get Nelson into hospital at Freetown. What about you, Anderson?'

To their surprise the planter elected to stay, as the only thing wrong with him, he averred, was fever, which he could soon put right if he could get at his quinine. His bungalow was only a mile or two away.

While they were waiting he told of how Griggs had come to him with a proposition for putting up the price of his produce. The man claimed he knew of a better market and had powerful friends behind him. Anderson, knowing the man's reputation, would have nothing to do with it, whereupon Griggs had bribed the witch-doctor to cause trouble in the plantations – an old trick – and then, while he was down with a bout of fever, made him a prisoner and carried him to the hut where they had found him. Nelson, who Griggs said was a spy, was brought in later.

Biggles nodded. 'That's about how my chief in London had it worked out. What surprises me is that they didn't murder you.'

'That's what they were doing, in slow time, when you rolled up,' stated the Scot. 'They daren't kill me outright for fear my boys would talk and the tale reach the Coast. All they had to do was withhold my quinine so that I died of fever. That would have been a natural death. I've quinine in the house, but as these crooks have been living in it I don't suppose there will be much left in the way of food.'

'I'll fly you out some stores from Freetown if you'll let me know what you want,' promised Biggles. 'What about this produce of yours? There's a fair load here. As I shall be going back to England with an empty machine would you like me to take it?'

'I'd be glad if you would, for having had half my crop pinched my finances will be pretty low. Dump it at any airport. I'll give you the name of my London agent. Let him know and he'll collect it. I must get on with my work here. With that rascal of a witch-doctor out of the way my boys will be all right. They've had no pay for months – not a penny since Griggs took over.'

It was left at that.

Biggles flew the French party to Kankan and then went on with Nelson to Freetown where he saw him safely into hospital. And it may be said here that he soon made a complete recovery. What had happened to him was much as had been surmised. Having located the airstrip he had been caught before he could get clear to make his report.

Having loaded the Wellington with the stores Anderson had asked for, Biggles flew them to the airstrip from where they were carried by the blacks to the bungalow, which was found to be in the state the planter had expected. They spent a few days with him helping to put the place in order. When that had been done, the produce that was to have been shipped in the Samson was loaded into the Wellington and taken to London, where in due course it was collected by Anderson's agent.

That is not quite the end of the story, for it transpired that from Kankan Marcel contacted the authorities at Bouflé, with the result that when the Samson landed there the police were waiting.

Convicted on the serious charge of wounding a policeman the surviving members of the gang are now doing some really hard work in a French penal battalion.

7

BIGGLES MAKES A BET

When Biggles walked into the office of his French opposite number, at the Sûreté in Paris, he was greeted with a smile and the remark: 'Ah! The old dog himself. You come hot of the foot, eh?'

'I seem to go through life hot-foot,' answered Biggles sadly, as they shook hands. 'You said you wanted to see me. Here I am. What's your trouble?'

'*My* trouble. *La la.* I think perhaps it is your trouble.'

Biggles took a seat and lit a cigarette. 'Tell me about it,' he requested.

'*Bon.* Two weeks ago one of your smart English boys, named Peter Keston, age nineteen, steals a light plane from the Lotton Flying Club after dark to give himself a ride – a joy-ride as he calls it.'

'I remember.'

'He loses his way, arrives in France, and bursts a tyre trying to land. Then, very bravely, he gives himself up. We send him home. You know about this?'

'Of course. He had never been at the controls before. He had no money, but being crazy to fly he helped himself to a plane.'

'That is what he told the judge who gave him a

month in prison for being a naughty boy. One little month for stealing an expensive aeroplane. Why does he only have a month when another silly fellow gets twelve months for stealing five pounds? I will tell you. Because, says the judge, it was a sporting effort to fly without lessons. You English are sport mad. *Tiens-tiens*. In England sport can turn a criminal into a hero. Tell me, *mon ami*, did you believe this story?'

'What story?'

'This flying without lessons.'

Biggles shrugged. 'I didn't check up on it seeing no reason. After all, it may have been a silly escapade but it needed nerve.'

Marcel shook his head sadly. 'So you, too, fall for this sporting effort talk. Sport makes you blind. Did you come in your Auster to France?'

'Yes. It's at Le Bourget.'

'Good. Then let us go. I want to show you something.'

An hour later the Auster was cruising over the River Marne, Biggles at the controls with Marcel indicating the route. 'The village you see in front is Charmentray. Then there is a big wood with a thin field running far into it.'

'I see it.'

'It was at the far end of that little field between the trees that your sportsman landed. Why did he choose such a place when there are big open fields all round?'

'Probably got into a panic and was glad to get down anywhere.'

'It was perhaps more sporting to land in the most difficult place,' returned Marcel sarcastically. 'Now you land in the same field. I will show you the exact spot where our young friend touched down.'

Biggles made a trial run and overshot. He tried again and nearly hit the trees. 'The wind's wrong,' he said. 'I can't get in.'

Said Marcel, smoothly, 'The wind is the same direction and force as the night your sporting boy landed. Now it is daylight and you tell me you can't get in! *Mot de Cambronne!* Don't tell me an old fox like you can't do in daylight what a boy on his first solo can do by night!'

Biggles frowned. He made three more false runs before, by skimming the trees in a steep sideslip, he managed to get his wheels on the ground. He drew a deep breath as the machine ran to a stop.

Marcel threw him a sidelong glance. 'You agree that boy was what you call a lucky lad,' he said softly, but meaningly.

Biggles nodded. 'Yes,' he said shortly. 'I get it. No one but a pilot of experience could get in here, and even he'd have to know the ground pretty well to tackle it by night. In fact, an experienced pilot would have more sense than to attempt it – unless he had a very good reason.'

'*Exactement!* That is what I thought you would think. It begins to look, does it not, as if your young sportsman lies as well as he flies.'

Biggles did not answer.

Went on Marcel, 'I must ask you, please, to tell me why this countryman of yours comes to my country by night.'

'I'd like to know that myself,' replied Biggles. 'He said he lost his way.'

Marcel laughed scornfully. 'So with an airfield not far away, and a choice of big fields, he lands in a wood. It won't do, my friend.'

Biggles looked at his smiling companion and smiled back.

'You win,' he conceded. 'My fault for not checking up – and here am I, always talking about never taking anything for granted.'

'What now?'

'I'll go and have a word with this young man,' declared Biggles grimly. 'He's still in gaol so I shall know where to find him.'

He taxied into the open, turned into wind and took off.

Back in England, the same afternoon, having shown his authority, he was admitted to the cell in which the culprit was under detention and left alone with him.

'Keston,' he began, 'as one pilot to another I want you to tell me why you flew to France the other night.'

The prisoner, a fair, good-looking lad, considered him suspiciously. 'I don't know what you mean?'

'Going to stick to the story, eh?'

'I've said my piece. It was a bit of fun. I just wondered if I could handle a plane.'

'It must be some time since you wondered that, laddie,' returned Biggles. 'I was flying before you were born and I've been at the game ever since, but it took me all my time to get down where you did without a crack-up.' He smiled. 'In other words, you handled that machine a bit too well. It doesn't go with the tale you told the court. Why not come clean?'

'I wanted to fly. That's the honest truth.'

'I believe that – for a beginning. Carry on. Let's have the rest.'

'I was half-way to my commercial ticket, and through no fault of my own ran out of money.'

Biggles shook his head sadly. 'So you pinched a plane.'

'I only borrowed it for a little while.'

'For what purpose?'

'To put in some night-flying practice.'

'You think that's the way to get a commercial licence. It won't do, Keston.'

'I couldn't see any other way.'

'Go on as you've started and all the flying you'll do will be between stone walls.'

'If I hadn't cut my tyre on that flint no one would have known about it.'

'You'd just have flown home again.'

'Sure,' confessed Keston, frankly.

'Having done what you went to France to do.'

'Sure.'

'Where did you get this sure stuff? Been reading American comics?'

'Sure.'

Biggles grinned. 'Okay, if that's how you want it. I've reason to believe you've the makings of a top-grade pilot. Maybe I could help you. Here's my card. Think it over. If you feel like coming over with the whole truth let me know. Cigarette?'

'Thanks.' Keston looked at the card. 'Bigglesworth, eh. I've heard of you. If I spill the beans will you get me out of here?'

'No. You'll serve your time. You deserved more than you got. I'll see you when you're discharged.'

'I wouldn't make it any worse for myself?'

'No. You've had your sentence.'

'Okay. I did it for a bet. I was hanging about the airfield when a slick American type asked me if I could fly. I said yes. He said he didn't believe it and offered to bet me fifty quid I couldn't fly to France and back. Needing money I took him on. To prove I'd been to France, he said, I'd have to hand a letter to a pal of his who'd be waiting, showing a red light, at a certain spot, and bring an answer back. I said okay. Not having a plane I borrowed one.'

'And the pal was at the other end to meet you?'

'Sure.'

'And you gave him the letter?'

'I'd call it a packet.'

'Did you get the answer?'

'No. The bloke faded as soon as he saw I'd burst a tyre and couldn't get home.'

'And left you holding the baby. Nice pal. You knew what you were doing?'

'Of course.'

'Did you get your fifty pounds?'

'Twenty. I was to have the other thirty when I got back.'

'What did you do with the twenty?'

'Hid it in a rabbit hole where I landed. Knowing it's illegal to export sterling I daren't be caught with it on me. In giving myself up I gambled on a light sentence.'

'Quite a gambler, aren't you? All right. Now I'll make a bet. A fiver you don't know the name or address of your pal.'

'No bet. He forgot to tell me.'

'Very well. Then I'll wager you never see the colour of your other thirty pounds – and I'll fetch your twenty from France into the bargain.'

A slow smile spread over Keston's face. 'I get it. You want to see me meet the guy. Nothing doing. If he comes across with the thirty quid he owes me I'll not rat on him. If he doesn't, I'm your man.'

'Fair enough.' Biggles got up. 'When your pal fails to turn up you'll find me at the Yard. So long for now.'

A fortnight later there was a knock on the door of the Air Police Operations Room. Keston walked in.

Biggles smiled. 'So he didn't pay.'

'No, the coyote.'

'He took you to the cleaners and left you to take the rap. Nice pal.' Biggles took from a drawer some five-pound notes. 'Here's the money you left in France.'

'Thanks.' Keston peeled off a note and offered it to Biggles.

Biggles' eyebrows went up. 'What's that for?'

'The bet was a fiver he didn't pay. Well, he hasn't paid, so I lose. When I lose I pay.'

Biggles brushed the note aside. 'Keep it. I like my money clean.'

'Then what was the idea of the bet?'

'The idea was, if this crook didn't pay, you'd help me to find him – and make *him* pay.'

'I'd make him pay on my own account if I could find him.'

'Fair enough, Keston. That's what I mean – we'll do the job together.'

'And how will you find him?'

'I'll tell you. Listen. This crook pulled a fast one on you. He's probably done it before. But whether he has

E

or whether he hasn't, as it's come off he'll try it again. I know what I'm talking about and you can take my word for it. That's why I'm here. The chances are that at this very moment your pal is looking for another poor sap to do his dirty work for him.'

'Okay. I was a sucker. I know it, but don't rub it in.'

'If I'm right your pal will be hanging round another airfield. Not the same one. He might run into you. You say you're crazy to fly. All right. Now you can go ahead. Ginger, my assistant, who is standing by you, will fly you round all the clubs in the country until you spot your man. If you're nice to him and don't try any funny stuff maybe Ginger will let you do a spot of aviation.'

'What happens if I see the guy?'

'All you have to do is point him out to Ginger. He'll do the rest. What you must not do is let the fellow see you.'

'I get it. But what about the thirty quid he owes me?'

'You might as well forget about that. He's no intention of paying or he'd have paid.'

'Maybe he couldn't find me to give it to me.'

'He could have sent it by post, couldn't he? Your name and address, with your photo, were in the newspapers, so he knew what had happened to you. Don't fool yourself that he ever intended paying. Anyway, after what you did I doubt if you're entitled to the money – from the official aspect. It was a bribe to make you break the law.'

'That's okay by me. When do we start aviating?'

'As the weather's fine, now. By the way, do I understand this man was an American?'

'He talked like one.'

'I believe there's an American camp near Lotton, where he picked you up?'

'Yes.'

Biggles turned to Ginger. 'Start with the flying club fields near American camps.'

'Right. Come on, Keston. Let's get mobile.'

It was four days before Biggles heard from either of them. Then Keston walked into the Ops. Room alone.

Biggles raised his eyebrows. 'Where's Ginger?'

'On the trail. We found the guy watching the flying on the Cliverton Club airfield. There's an American camp close by so your idea worked out. Ginger sent me home by train to report, saying he was going to try something.'

'What do you reckon he meant by that?'

'He said he'd watch the guy to see if he picked up another mug, but I've an idea he was hoping to be picked up himself.'

'Ah!' breathed Biggles. 'If that comes off the next we shall hear from him will be on the high frequency radio. You can stick around if you like. I may need you for evidence of identification.'

Algy was on radio duty when, the same night, after dark, the signal came through.

'Ginger's on his way to France with a packet,' he reported to Biggles.

'Great work. What's his objective?'

'Charmentray – the same landing ground as Keston. A red light will mark the actual spot.'

Biggles frowned. 'I hope Ginger gets in all right. It isn't easy.'

'What's the idea of choosing such a tricky place?'

'To keep under cover of the trees, I suppose. I can't imagine any other reason. The country around is open and a plane landing would be seen.'

'Ah-ha. Ginger wants to know the drill. Is he to carry on?'

Biggles thought for a moment. 'He's by himself?'

'Yes.'

'We can't let him handle the job single-handed. It's too dangerous. Besides, he can't make arrests in France. Tell him to land at Le Bourget and wait for me there. I shall have to speak to Marcel and ask him how he wants this handled. When you've spoken to Ginger you might get the Sûreté for me on the private line.'

'Fair enough.'

It was nearly three hours later when the police Auster arrived over the Charmentray rendezvous. In it were Biggles, Ginger, and Marcel Brissac, of the French Air Police.

'There's the red light,' observed Ginger. 'The thing begins to look like a piece of cake.'

'Provided I can get down without breaking anything,' answered Biggles. 'It's a bit trappy. Fortunately, I've done it once.'

A few minutes later the Auster's wheels touched down without mishap. Said Biggles, 'Let me go first. If he sees more than one he may take fright.' He got out alone.

A man at once emerged from the gloom and hurried towards him.

'Is this what you're waiting for?' queried Biggles, holding out a bulky envelope.

'Sure. And you can take this back with you,' was the crisp answer.

The man put a small parcel into Biggles' hands.

'Thanks,' said Biggles.

'That's all. So long.' The man turned to go.

Biggles caught him by the arm. 'Not quite all,' he snapped. 'I'm a police officer, and I . . .'

'You –' snarled the man, tearing his arm free. He started to run. Biggles tripped him and he fell.

By this time Marcel and Ginger were on the scene. As the man scrambled to his feet a pistol blazed from his hip. Ginger grabbed the arm that held the gun, but it took all three of them to hold him until the handcuffs were on his wrists. Then some men whom Marcel had sent down by road ran up and that settled the matter.

Biggles opened the packet that had been given to Ginger for delivery and showed the contents to Marcel.

Marcel, panting, holding a blood-stained handkerchief to his cheek, addressed the cursing prisoner grimly. 'For importing counterfeit dollar bills you would have gone to prison for a long time. For shooting a police officer you will go for a much longer time. Take him away.'

'Let's see what sort of contraband he was sending to England,' suggested Biggles, cutting open the small parcel that had been handed to him. 'Cigarettes,' he muttered, looking at the contents.

Marcel sniffed them. 'Marijuana! Enough to dope a fair-sized community. I wonder who they were intended for.'

'I think I know,' answered Biggles. 'I'll take them with me, if you don't mind, and confirm it. I'll drop you at Le Bourget on the way. It's time a doctor had a look at your face. You had a close shave that time.'

'*Pst*. A scratch,' said Marcel, as he got into the machine.

There were three people, apart from Air Commodore Raymond, chief of the Air Police, in his headquarters office at Scotland Yard. They were Biggles, senior operational pilot, Air Constable 'Ginger' Hebblethwaite, and Colonel Dawson, a staff security officer of the United States Air Force in Britain. The Air Commodore was speaking to the American.

'I've called you in because I think you should know about this,' he said. 'If my senior pilot's suspicions are correct I shall need your co-operation. Briefly, the story is this. Bigglesworth here, working with the French representative of the International Police Commission, has uncovered an illicit air shuttle service between this country and France. Until we stepped in it was being run by two Americans. There must be others in it. It may have been going on for some time. We don't know. But we're on the way to putting an end to the traffic.'

'What was the racket?' asked the American officer.

'Spurious dollar bills were going from this country to France, by air. The pilot of the aircraft was bringing back cigarettes. Here is a sample of them.' The Air Commodore indicated a box of cigarettes that lay on his desk.

The security officer selected a cigarette and examined it. 'There doesn't appear to be anything wrong with this,' he observed. 'It's a common enough brand.'

'The brand may be common but the dope that has

been put in them is not, thank goodness,' returned the
Air Commodore, grimly. 'It's marijuana. You don't
need me to tell you what effect it has on the people who
smoke the stuff. These particular cigarettes are faked,
of course. I mean, they were never made by the
people whose trade mark is on them, for which reason,
aside from any other, they could do the firm a great
deal of harm.'

'Sure. Do you know the name of the operator on this
side of the Channel?'

'Yes.'

'American?'

'Yes.'

'Civilian?'

'Yes.'

'Then go ahead and pick him up. The United States
government will thank you. I'm only concerned with
the army, not civilians.'

'That brings us to the reason why I asked you to
come here,' averred the Air Commodore. 'The man
importing these coffin nails may be a civilian, but it
doesn't necessarily follow that his customers are.'

'What are you getting at?'

'We know for certain that the operator, the importer
of this stuff, is working round American airfields in this
country, which suggests that his customers are United
States military personnel. It's only a suggestion, mind
you! Have you noticed any unusual behaviour among
your pilots or air crews?'

The American stared at the Air Commodore, a
curious expression dawning in his eyes. 'My God!' he
breathed. 'I wonder if that's the answer.'

'To what?'

'Some of our boys have been doing the craziest things lately – low flying and lunatic stunting – with the result that we've had an ugly crop of crack-ups. There's also been a lot of rowdyism, fighting, and so on, for no reason that we've been able to discover. Of course, we know that with nothing much to do fellers are liable to get browned off, but even so, we've been a bit puzzled to account for what's been going on.'

'Well, if your men have discovered a cure for boredom in marijuana that might well be the answer to your problem. You know it reacts.'

'Sure. The stuff has the reputation of eliminating fear, which is why it was used by professional killers in our days of gang warfare. The stuff was introduced from Mexico. We suspected that something was wrong, and as you say, this may be the answer. What are you going to do about it? I can't check every carton of cigarettes to see if they're right or phoney. That of course was the object in putting the stuff in one of our most common brands.'

'Until we have actual proof that your fellows are involved I think you'd better leave this in our hands,' said the Air Commodore, thoughtfully. 'Not a word to anyone except perhaps station commanders, who had better know in case there's trouble.'

'Okay, if you say so,' agreed the American. 'This is your country. I'll get along. Thanks for giving me the tip.'

After the Colonel had gone the Air Commodore looked at Biggles. 'Well, what's the next move?'

'We've got to catch this dope merchant red-handed,' answered Biggles. 'I imagine he'll still be hanging around the Cliverton Flying Club waiting for Ginger to come back to collect his fee – and hand over the cigarettes. We could pick him up, there and then, but we still wouldn't know for certain where the stuff has been going, or where the phoney dollar bills are coming from.'

'What do you suggest?'

Biggles considered the matter for a moment. 'The best plan, I think, is to fill this box with ordinary cigarettes. The box itself will smell enough of marijuana to prevent any suspicion of a switch. Ginger can go to Cliverton, find his man and hand the box over, explaining the delay by saying he had engine trouble. I'll be there, but I'd like two of Inspector Gaskin's professional sleuths on hand to do any shadowing that may have to be done. As soon as we know where the dope is going I'll step in and pick up this dope pedlar.'

'All right. I'll leave it to you.'

When, later in the day, Ginger landed his Auster on the Cliverton aerodrome, Biggles was already there, in the clubhouse, talking to the bar steward, an ex-R.A.F. man whom he had known in the Service. At that hour there were only a few people in the lounge. One, an American by his drawl, who seemed to be on familiar terms with everyone, was standing drinks.

'Who's the gent with the natty neckwear?' Biggles asked the steward, softly.

'American named Caulder, sir. He's often here.'

'How did he get in? Is he a member of the club?'

'Some of the pilots at the camp are honorary members. One brought this chap in one evening and he's been drifting in ever since. The secretary doesn't think much of him but doesn't like to do anything about it for fear of upsetting the camp.'

Caulder walked suddenly to the window and Biggles knew why. Ginger had landed and was taxi-ing in. Caulder went out. Biggles followed, and took up a position from which he could hear the conversation when they met.

'So you got it,' said Caulder eagerly. 'Nice work. I was getting worried about you.'

'Had to drop in at Lympne with a sticky valve,' answered Ginger casually, handing over the package he carried.

'Thanks a lot,' said Caulder, and turned away.

'Just a minute,' called Ginger. 'What about – what you promised me?'

'Sorry. I haven't got it on me right now.'

'What's the idea. Is this a double-cross?'

'What if it was?'

'I could tell the police –'

Caulder laughed harshly. 'And put yourself in the pen? Think it over, brother.' He walked to a sports car and drove off. Another car followed.

'That cheap crook,' said Ginger disgustedly, when he joined Biggles.

Biggles smiled. 'Don't worry. His game's about played out. Let's go in and have some tea.'

Just after six the car that had followed Caulder returned and Biggles joined the plain-clothes man who had driven it. Said the driver, a policeman: 'He's in the village, in the bar of the Black Horse, selling gaspers to American flyers at five dollars a time. My mate is watching him.'

'Capital. Ring the Camp Commandant and ask

him to hurry to the Black Horse. I'll borrow your car.'

For a moment, as they entered the village inn, Ginger thought Biggles' plan had miscarried. Voices were raised in anger. Cigarettes lay on the floor. Caulder, looking agitated, for he was being threatened, was protesting.

'Looks as if the boys object to paying five bucks for ordinary tobacco,' Biggles told Ginger quietly.

For a few minutes, until they heard the skid of tyres outside, they watched the scene. Then Biggles walked up to the dope pedlar. 'I'm a police officer,' he announced, 'and –' the rest was lost in the hubbub as a general rush was made for the door. It died abruptly to silence as the U.S. Station Commandant, with military police behind him, blocked the way.

'Take it easy,' ordered the officer, crisply. His eyes went round the room, taking in the scene. They came to rest on Caulder. Recognition dawned. He made a gesture to his escort and pointed. 'Arrest that man!' he barked.

Biggles introduced himself. 'You know what this is all about, sir?'

'Yes. I was told on the phone this morning by our Security Headquarters.'

'You seemed to know that man in civvies who calls himself Caulder.'

'I'd say I do,' came back the Commandant curtly. 'He deserted from my squadron when we were with the occupation forces in Germany.'

Biggles smiled faintly. 'That,' he said evenly, shouldn't make the next few years any easier for him.'

8

MURDER BY THIRST

BIGGLES looked up from his desk as a Scotland Yard messenger entered the Air Police office and announced that 'two young people' wished to see him.

'What do they want to see me about?' asked Biggles.

'They say they'd rather tell you personally.'

'All right. Show them in.'

The two young people entered and the messenger retired. One was a tall fair boy of perhaps seventeen; the other, a girl, somewhat younger.

'What can I do for you?' inquired Biggles.

The boy answered, a trifle nervously. 'Are you the famous Biggles?'

Biggles smiled faintly. 'Well, let's say I'm Biggles, anyway. Who are you?'

'My name's John Murray and this is Sally Dunn. I come from Kalgoorlie and Sally lives in Perth. We arrived from Australia by air a week ago to finish our studies at the London School of Music. There's something we feel you ought to know about.'

'Sit down and go ahead.' Ginger pulled up two chairs.

Sally nudged her companion. 'You tell him,' she prompted.

John began. 'About four months ago there arrived in Western Australia an Englishman, an elderly man, name of Mr Farlow. It seems he'd always had an ambition to go prospecting for gold, and now he'd retired from business and had some money he'd come to Australia for that purpose. People got to know about him through an advertisement he put in the newspaper. He knew nothing about the practical side of prospecting although he had some theories; and, of course, he didn't know the country, so he was looking for a partner who did. The idea was, he'd pay all expenses and they'd share any profit.'

'That was sensible of him, anyway.'

'Yes. But he should have taken advice about the man he chose, for he couldn't have found a worse one. It was a well-known bad character named Black Jack Barnes. I knew him by sight; so did Sally. He'd been in prison more than once. He was usually drunk and looking for a fight with someone – anyone.'

'Why did no one warn Mr Farlow that this fellow was a wrong-un?'

'No one knew about it until too late. They'd gone. My father was angry about it. When word went round that Mr Farlow had been seen going off with Barnes in a jeep people said they should have been stopped. My father thought Barnes must have seen the advertisement, saw Mr Farlow, and persuaded him to keep quiet about the trip, knowing jolly well that someone would tip Mr Farlow off as to what sort of man he was. Anyway, they went off; and they never came back; which in one way was surprising because Black Jack was an experienced digger and knew the country well enough.'

'Then what?'

'After some weeks had passed without sign of them an air search was started. The jeep had been seen heading for the waterless country to the north-east and it couldn't carry enough water to stay in the desert indefinitely. After some time a plane spotted it in the wild country south-west of the Musgrave Ranges. The pilot went down and found it bogged to the chassis in soft mud. The tanks were dry. Of Mr Farlow and Barnes there was no sign. They were never found.'

'A search was made for them, I imagine?'

'Yes. A police tracker was flown out but he reckoned the jeep had been abandoned for a month. There had been some wind, and sand had blown over any trail there might have been. There was a lot of talk, of course. How came the jeep to be so far out? How came an old hand like Barnes to get stuck? – and so on. But there was no proof of anything crooked and eventually the talk fizzled out. It was assumed that the two men had started to walk and had perished, as has happened more than once in that country. They were more than a hundred miles from the nearest water.'

'Their bodies weren't found?'

'No, Barnes wasn't found for a good reason. He's here, in London.'

Biggles sat up in his chair. 'Are you sure of that?'

'Certain. He boarded our plane at Darwin, togged up in new clothes. I said to Sally you know who that is, and she said yes, it's Black Jack Barnes. When we saw his left hand we knew there was no mistake because he'd lost the two end fingers fusing a stick of dynamite to blast some rock.'

'He came to London with you?'

'Yes.'

'How long have you been here?'

'A week. I wrote at once to my father; but as Barnes was in London, and we'd read about you, we decided to tell you.'

Biggles' eyes met those of the boy. 'What's *your* idea of what happened?'

'We asked ourselves some questions. How did Barnes, who was always broke, get the money to come here? Again, *why* has he come to London?'

'You think he may have found what he was looking for – gold?'

'Yes. But that doesn't quite add up to make sense. He wouldn't be able to carry any quantity of ore, on foot, with food and water for at least a hundred miles across bad country. If he made a strike why didn't he stake his claim and have it recorded in the ordinary way?'

'You tell me.'

'Because if he had people would have said, what about your partner? Where's Mr Farlow? That might have been an awkward question to answer. I'd say it was because he didn't want to answer it that he never came back to Kalgoorlie. Neither has Mr Farlow come back. His luggage has never been collected.'

'In other words, you think Barnes may have murdered Farlow?'

'He must have had a good reason for not recording his claim.'

'Assuming he had one to record.'

'If he didn't make a strike how did he get the money to come to London? And why come here, anyway? It's my guess that he struck something big; too big to handle alone; in which case he'd try to get one of the mining companies interested. He wouldn't dare to do that in Australia, but here, where nobody knows him, he'd be safe.'

Biggles smiled. 'I see you've got this all worked out.'

'Sally and I have talked of nothing else for a week. We think you should find Barnes and ask him what happened to your fellow countryman Farlow. If he's dead, even if Barnes didn't kill him he must know how and where he died.'

'He'll have the answer ready, no doubt.'

'If he says Farlow died ask him where he buried the body. In Australia a man doesn't leave his partner lying about for dingo meat.'

'All right. Let's leave it at that for the moment,' said Biggles, rising. 'You did right to report this. Give me a description of Barnes and let me have your addresses so that I can get in touch with you should it be necessary.'

'I can show you a photo of Barnes,' said John, surprisingly.

Biggles' eyebrows went up. 'How did you get that?'

'Sally had her camera in the plane. She took a snap-shot of him when he was asleep. She wanted to send it home to prove he was on the plane.'

'Pretty good,' complimented Biggles. 'That was clever of you.'

After the young Australians had gone he turned to Ginger. 'Buzz Inspector Gaskin on the intercom. and ask him if he'd oblige me by stepping up here for a minute.'

Presently the burly criminal detective came. 'What's

on your mind?' he growled, tapping out his pipe in Biggles' ash-tray.

'I want you to do a little job for me, if you will. You've men to handle it. I haven't, without wasting a lot of time. It's quite simple. A week ago an Australian named Barnes arrived here by air. Here's a photo of him. I want discreet inquiries made round the gold mining companies to find out if he has called on them and if so for what purpose. I'd start with the companies having interests in Australia. He'd be most likely to know their names.'

'That shouldn't take long,' said the Inspector, putting the photograph in his notebook. 'That all?'

'For the moment, yes, thanks.'

'Okay.'

Gaskin departed, but was back the same evening. 'Did you want to have a word with this feller Barnes?'

'Yes.'

'Then you're too late. He's on his way back, with a mining engineer and surveyor, in a plane belonging to the Antipodes Mining Corporation.'

Biggles stared. 'By thunder! He must have had a tale to tell to induce the company to move as fast as that, and spend what the trip will cost.'

Gaskin drew on his pipe. 'He showed them samples of quartz so stuffed with gold that if he's telling the truth when he says he knows where there's tons of it, there may be millions involved.'

'That certainly lets in a broad beam of daylight,' said Biggles softly. 'Those kids were right. Thanks, Gaskin. When did this plane leave?'

'Yesterday.'

'Fine. With luck we might still beat it to Australia.

I'll go and have a word with the Air Commodore. I think he'll agree that a run to Australia is indicated.'

A week later found the Air Police Wellington heading out over the lonely wastelands that comprise so much of Western Australia. Sitting beside Biggles in the cockpit, acting as guide, was the police sergeant who had been with the search party when the jeep was found. At police headquarters Biggles had repeated the story told by the two young Australians, revealed what he had learned subsequently, and this was the result. The journey out had been uneventful, without sign of the gold company's aircraft. Stopping only for fuel Biggles thought, and hoped, that he had arrived first.

He had of course discussed the affair at some length with the Australian police officials but had learned little more than he already knew. The jeep had been examined without yielding any clue as to what had happened. Farlow had not been found, alive or dead, although considering the nature of the country this surprised nobody.

Biggles was hoping that the body of the amateur gold hunter might still be found, although, as he admitted freely to the sergeant, it was a forlorn hope; for if Barnes had in fact murdered his partner, and buried the body, it would be futile to search for it. There was still some doubt about the murder theory, the weak part being the motive; for if the prospectors had by a lucky chance 'struck it rich' there would have been no reason for Barnes to kill his companion, since there would have been ample wealth for both of them.

One important factor in favour of the employment

of an aircraft for the present purpose was the occurrence, as the sergeant had assured Biggles, of plenty
of places where a landing could be made – at all events,
in the open country where the jeep was found. The
terrain was flat, mostly sand or stony desert and free
from obstructions except those which could be seen,
such as areas of spinifex or clumps of shrubby mulga.
In general, the panorama, as it lay shimmering under
the merciless sun, was one of inhospitable monotony.
The superheated air was thin, and the aircraft rocked
in the bumps.

The sergeant indicated a ridge of blue hills that had
crept up over the horizon. 'Those are the Musgraves.
We found the jeep in a drift just this side of them.
As you see, there's plenty of room to land if you want
to.'

'And there's plenty of room for a man to get lost in,'
returned Biggles, grimly. 'A man stranded here would,
I imagine, head west?'

'That's the nearest way to water even though it's a
long way off.'

'How long, here, could a man last without water?'

'He wouldn't get far. A couple of days in this blistering wilderness would about finish him. How long do
you reckon to stay here?'

'Until Barnes comes. I look at it like this. He found
gold. That we know. He'll come back. The place where
he made the strike can't be far from where the jeep
was found, so if we sit down we should either see him
or hear the aircraft when it arrives. This is the one
place where, sooner or later, we can be sure of finding
him.'

'There's the place where we found the jeep.' The

sergeant pointed out. 'You can still see the mark where we hauled it out.'

Biggles took the aircraft down nearly to ground level, circled twice, but did not land. Speaking over the intercom. he told the others, who were aft, to watch for anything like a body; and with that he started quartering in a westerly direction. This was continued for half an hour, when the sergeant said, in his opinion, Farlow couldn't have got as far even if he had started in good shape.

Biggles turned. 'A man, knowing he was finished, wouldn't just sit down on the open ground and die,' he opined. 'He'd look for cover of some sort if only to get out of the sun. The only shade I can see is that clump of mulga ahead. It might be worth spending a couple of minutes having a look at it.'

The sergeant gave Biggles a curious look but said nothing.

Biggles landed close to the trees, switched off, stepped down and lit a cigarette while the others joined him. He then led the way to the sun-scorched mulga and walked on into the deepest shade. Suddenly he stopped. 'That, I fancy, is all that's left of the man we're looking for,' he said quietly, pointing to some shrivelled, mummified remains lying against a stump.

In the silence that followed the sergeant went on and for a minute or two was busy. 'It's him,' he said briefly, rising. 'I found this note in his pocket. Let's see what he has to say.' He unfolded a small piece of paper. As he read it his brow darkened. 'So now we know,' he said shortly, when he had finished. 'He must have hoped that someone would find him, one day.'

'What happened?'

'He says they found gold, a vein of quartz so rich that the metal was sticking out of it. On the way home to register their claims, Barnes, who was driving, by accident or design stuck the jeep in a sand drift. They were already short of water, but there was nothing else for it but to start walking. The first night out, Farlow says, while he was asleep, Barnes went off taking all the remaining water with him. He woke up to find himself alone. Knowing he hadn't a hope of getting back he wrote this letter and crept into the only bit of shade to die.'

Biggles dropped his cigarette end and put his heel on it. 'I don't know what the law is in this country but if Barnes took all the water knowing his partner must die of thirst, then he killed him just as surely as if he had put a bullet through his head.'

'That's how it looks to me, and what most people will say,' agreed the sergeant in a hard voice. He raised a hand. 'Hark! That's a plane coming now. It can only be Barnes.'

Standing in the fringe of the scrub they watched the machine pass overhead, watched it till the engines died and it circled down to land on the edge of the foothills of the mountain range.

'Let's go over,' said the sergeant, crisply.

There was no one with the aircraft as they landed beside it, the pilot apparently having gone with the others to see the claim, so they sat in the shade of a wing to wait. They waited for nearly two hours before Barnes and the others returned. There was a brief hesitation on the part of Barnes when he saw the sergeant's uniform but he came on with the others, having no alternative.

'Barnes,' said the sergeant sternly, 'I want a word with you.'

'Mr Barnes is a lucky man,' said one of the surveyors.

'That's what you think, and maybe what he thinks.'

'He's made a strike that will cause a sensation.'

'It'll cause a sensation all right,' returned the sergeant, caustically. He faced the prospector squarely. 'Where's Mr Farlow?'

'He died of snake-bite,' lied Barnes glibly. 'He would wander off by himself. I did what I could for him but it was no use.'

'Then what?'

'I buried him, of course.'

'Where?'

Barnes made a vague sweep with an arm. 'Over there. I couldn't say exactly where.'

'You needn't try,' sneered the sergeant. 'We've found him. Before he died he wrote a letter, and the story it tells is a different one from yours. The court can decide which is the right one. You're coming back with me.'

Barnes' dark eyes roamed the landscape as if he contemplated making a bolt for it. But all around, as he must have realized, lay the death to which he had condemned his partner. His hand moved towards his pocket, but it stopped when he found himself looking into the muzzle of Biggles' gun.

'Come on,' cracked the sergeant. 'You gentlemen had better get back to England and forget what's happened here,' he added, with a glance at the speechless surveyors. 'I'm sorry if you've come a long way for nothing.'

Handcuffs clicked on the prisoner's wrists.

'After we've dropped you off, sergeant, I think we'll push along home, too,' said Biggles. 'Don't forget to whom the credit for this is due. I'll see them when I get back.'

'I'll remember,' promised the sergeant.

9

A MATTER OF
DEDUCTION

BIGGLES replaced the Air Police operations room telephone receiver, made a note on his pad, and walked
over to the big wall maps of Western Europe.

'That sounded like Marcel Brissac of the Sûreté,'
said Ginger.

'It was,' confirmed Biggles. 'He wants us to go over.
He has a mess on his hands, and I gather he feels
there's more to it than meets the eye. Ring the secretary of the Holmwood Flying Club and tell him one
of his machines, Tiger Moth GB-XKZ, is down in
France, in small pieces. It didn't catch fire so the
papers are there to identify it. Get particulars. Who
was in the machine when it took off and at what time
did it leave the ground.'

'How many people were in it when it crashed?'

'One body, in the front seat.'

'You mean, dead?'

'Very dead. Name, according to documents in the
pockets, Dennis Crayford. Algy, check the list of
licence holders for the name. Bertie, you might try the
Air Force List. You may find him on Reserve. If so

try to get his record from the Air Ministry. Say it's urgent. You can tell them he's been killed in a crash. I'll be getting the Proctor out. No need for us all to go over. I'll take Ginger with me in case I need a second pilot.'

When Biggles came back a quarter of an hour later the information he had asked for was there. Ginger reported first. The Tiger Moth named, the property of the Club, had been reported missing. It had been taken up by a Club member at 8.0 p.m. the previous evening. Name, Dennis Crayford. Purpose; a night-flying training flight. Crayford was an ex-Flight Lieutenant R.A.F., trying for his civilian ticket. He had nearly finished his course. The briefing had been a solo flight to Gatwick and back. 'How on earth did he get to France in weather conditions that must have been near perfect?' concluded Ginger.

'Don't waste time guessing. Maybe that's what Marcel wants to know. Have you any news, Algy?'

'No. He isn't on the register of civil pilots.'

'We know that now. He was after his ticket. How about you, Bertie?'

'Dennis Adrian Crayford, aged twenty-nine. On Reserve. Three years an air gunner before getting his wings. Did three years as a single-seater fighter pilot in service squadrons before being transferred to Reserve for medical reasons.'

'Good. Now we know where we are.'

'But that's fantastic,' declared Ginger. 'Not even a pupil on his first solo, much less an experienced pilot, could lose his way to that extent in good visibility. He must have seen the Channel.'

'Of course he did. Quite obviously the pilot of that

flying machine had no intention of going to Gatwick. The aircraft didn't catch fire when it crashed because its tanks, with the exception of a little in gravity, were dry – so Marcel says. It looks as if the machine flew south as far as its fuel would take it and then crash-landed.'

'Where actually did that happen?'

'Not far from Provins, a small country market town on the main line south of Paris; which suggests that the pilot might have been following the railway when he ran out of juice. Marcel says if we follow the line we can't miss seeing the crash at the bottom end of a big grass field on the right-hand side of the track. Let's go. Take care of things till I get back, Algy. I shouldn't be long.'

As they walked towards the aircraft Ginger went on: 'Did Marcel give any particular reason for wanting us to go over? He'd been able to identify the machine and the pilot, so presumably the log books were there.'

'No. But I gather from what he said that he suspects there's something phoney about this crash. Apart from that, as the machine is one of ours, and had no business to be in France, he was bound to advise us. Had a French machine hit the deck on our side of the ditch I would have done the same thing. There are some queer goings-on nowadays, and the whole idea of Interpol was co-operation.'

'Does he know what time this crash occurred?'

'Apparently not. No one saw it happen. It was found by a farm labourer going to work shortly after day-light. It must have been there most of the night. I mean, if the Tiger left the ground at eight and flew straight there, as for the sake of argument we will assume it did, it must have hit the ground somewhere about ten. The engine was stone cold when Marcel got to it, anyway. I don't mean hit the ground literally. It ran head-on into a tree, which makes it look as if the pilot made a boob and overshot. He must have hit the tree pretty hard, too. Crayford was flying from the front seat, and the fuselage was so telescoped they had a job to get the body out.'

'That looks queer in itself — unless Crayford was drunk, or blind.'

'He may have dropped off to sleep. That's happened before today. I once did it myself on a long night run. I might never have known about it had I not had a dream. It may only have been for a few seconds, but when I realized what had happened it shook me to no small order. Luckily it was a calm night and the machine was still on course. Here we are.'

An hour and a half later, shortly before ten o'clock, after circling round the little crowd that had gathered near the crash, Biggles landed, taxied on to where Marcel stood waiting, switched off and jumped down.

'Well, here we are,' he greeted, as they shook hands. 'Any developments?'

'*Non.*'

Biggles indicated a significant-looking blanket near the crash. An ambulance was parked beside it. 'Is that the body?'

'*Oui.*'

'What's the idea of keeping it here?'

'I think you might like to see it.'

'That's not a nice way to start the day on a fine

morning. Have you a particular reason for wanting me to see it?'

'Yes. We may need supporting evidence, *mon ami*, and we cannot make evidence of what we have not seen.'

'What about the doctor? Is he here?'

'He has been, but must go because he has ill people to see.'

'He gave you a certificate?'

'Yes.'

'What does it say? If you tell me I shall know what to look for.'

'The pilot he is dead because the bone at the back of his head – how do you call it?'

'Skull.'

'*Exactement*. It is broken. Crushed like an egg which is dropped.'

'Did you say the *back* of his head?' Biggles was looking at the crash.

'*Oui*. The back. So you think that is *extraordinaire, hein*?'

'I'd say it's more than extraordinary,' answered Biggles slowly.

'That is what I think. And that is why, because this is an Englishman, I ask you to come quickly. All the men I have seen who die by running fast into a thing that is hard break the front of their heads. In an aeroplane there is glass in the face where it hits the instruments, because when the plane stops suddenly the pilot goes forward, not back. And as you see, this plane she stops very sudden – *pom*. This poor man dies not from the crash but because his skull is broken by a blow from behind.'

'You mean – there was someone in the back seat?'

'That is it.'

'But wait a minute. There was no one in the back seat when the machine hit the tree or he would have been hurt. I doubt if he was in the machine at all.'

'So! Now we have a mystery.'

'I'll tell you something else,' said Biggles, lighting a cigarette. 'This man Crayford was a pilot of experience. For three years he flew in the R.A.F. Therefore he must have known what every pilot knows, that it is better in case of collision to let the wings take the shock and so save the fuselage in which he sits. Why did this man apparently go to great pains to ram his nose into the trunk of a big tree at high speed? It would have been better to turn, even though he wrenched off the undercarriage.'

'He did not ram the tree, which he must have seen if he is alive, because he is already dead. Dead from a strike on the back of the skull.'

'That,' said Biggles, 'is the answer. The only answer. The answer I would expect from an intelligent detective like Marcel Brissac.'

'*Merci, monsieur.* Now tell me, old dog, what happens here last night?'

'After taking off, solo, in England, Crayford must have landed somewhere and picked up a passenger, one who was able to fly an aeroplane. As he had no licence he would not have been allowed to take off with one. In the air this passenger hits Crayford on the head with enough force to kill him. Perhaps he only means to stun him, but he kills him, so he must have struck hard. Having killed his pilot he flies this way, perhaps following the line which he would see plainly, until he has only enough petrol left to make a landing. Here is a big field – perfect. He lands. But he cannot leave the machine in the field with a dead man in it. It must look as if the pilot is killed in a crash. So he takes the machine near to this tree, opens the throttle wide and jumps off. When he goes away he leaves what he hopes the police will think is a genuine crash. Maybe he doesn't know that there are now police who also have experience of aviation.'

'That is the story,' confirmed Marcel. 'Now we must find this passenger who is a murderer.'

'That shouldn't take long.'

'France is a big country, *mon ami*, and our man has a long start.'

'The machine left the ground at eight o'clock last night. If we work on the assumption that it flew straight here, and we can do that as the murderer, by using all his petrol, clearly wanted to get as far south as possible, the landing here must have been made about ten o'clock.'

'Which means that our man may be hundreds of kilometres away by now.'

'How far he has got will depend on the mode of transport he employed. If this was a rendezvous, and someone met him here, he may be difficult, but by no means impossible, to find.'

'He could be out of France by now,' put in Ginger.

'He could, but I don't think he will,' answered Biggles. 'He would be taking a desperate risk if he tried it. No, he won't try to leave France – not just yet, anyway.'

'Why not?'

'You seem to have forgotten that in order to cross

a frontier you must produce a passport, which is
checked by the passport officers of both the countries
concerned – the country the traveller is leaving and the
one he is entering.'

'The murderer may have a passport.'

'Even so he'd be a fool to show it. Having made an
illegal entry into France it will show no *Entree* stamp,
with the date. How could he explain that? His
nationality doesn't alter the case.'

'*Bon,*' came back Marcel. 'We find this man with
a passport that is more dangerous than no passport
at all. Now tell me, old fox, where shall I start?'

'If the man wanted to go south by the quickest
means available there's the main line railway nice and
handy. That might be the very reason, to be near the
railway, that he chose this field. Suppose we have a
word with the stationmaster, or the booking-clerk, at
the station over the way? There can't have been many
passengers demanding tickets from such a small station
during the night. He may remember some of them.
Let's go over. You can ask the questions, Marcel.'

After telling the driver of the ambulance to remove
the body of the dead airman, and leaving a gendarme
in charge, Marcel led the way to the station, a mere ten
minutes' walk. Having found the *chef de gare*, who
happened to be in the booking-office, he proceeded
with his questions.

These produced the results Biggles had anticipated.
Three tickets only had been issued during the night;
two to people known to the booking-clerk for the next
station down the line, and the other to a stranger, for
Nice, on the Riviera. The clerk remembered this man
well, for he had had to wait a long time for his train.

They had spoken, and he had observed him closely, as is the way of country people, particularly as in this case the traveller spoke like a foreigner. An Englishman, he thought, from his accent. They seldom had tourists there and the clerk had wondered what he was doing. In fact, he had asked him, but received only a vague reply. He described the man as fair, well-built, about thirty years of age. He wore a check tweed cap, a light waterproof, and carried a leather portfolio. He had arrived, and asked for a ticket, at about half past ten.

Questions now turned to the times of trains.

'From this station the man would catch only a slow train?' said Marcel, to the stationmaster.

'Certainly, monsieur. In any case, the *Rapide* and the *Train Bleu* had already gone through. The expresses do not stop here.'

'At what time would he arrive at Nice?'

The stationmaster looked it up. 'At four o'clock this afternoon.'

'He might not go through to Nice,' Ginger pointed out. 'He could get out, say, at Marseilles.'

'That is possible,' conceded Biggles. 'But there would be a big difference in the fare between Marseilles and Nice, and if he booked to Nice the chances are that he intended going there. Being one of the largest cities in France it would be a good place to lie low, if that's the intention. Anyway, it's doubtful if we could get to Marseilles before him but we could certainly beat him to Nice. How about it, Marcel? Shall we fly down? To catch him coming off the train would be easier than looking for him later, when he has established himself in some small hotel or apartment.'

Marcel agreed, so having thanked the stationmaster for his assistance they returned to the scene of the crash.

'We might as well all fly down together in my machine,' suggested Biggles, and again Marcel concurred.

'I will give orders that nothing here is to be touched,' he said. 'There should be fingerprints, perhaps on the joy-sticks. If those of the gentleman who goes to Nice are found also on this aeroplane he will find it not easy to explain how it happened, eh, old fox? *Voila!* Let us go.'

They took off and headed south. Landing only once, at Bron airport, Lyons, for fuel, they arrived at Nice nearly an hour before the train was due. In fact, they thought they saw the train approaching Cannes, Biggles having deliberately gone a little out of his way to strike the coast west of Nice and so follow the railway to the objective. From the big modern airport of Nice a taxi took them to police headquarters, where Marcel, having explained the situation, was able to enlist the services of two gendarmes should they be required.

And so it came about that when the long train, grimy after its journey from Paris, drew into the vast station, five people were waiting at the barrier, the two uniformed policemen standing a little back from the others.

As they stood there watching the passengers alight Ginger could imagine what a shock was in store for the man they sought should he be among them, for by this time, having put many hundreds of miles between him and his victim he would be, not without reason, congratulating himself on a clean get-away. The odd thought struck Ginger that the man who had used an aeroplane to commit a crime was now likely to be brought to justice by the same means.

Most of the passengers had passed through the barrier, and Ginger was beginning to wonder if their scheme had after all misfired, when Biggles said quietly: 'Here he comes.'

There was no mistaking the man, for the description they had been given fitted in every detail. Swinging the portfolio, his light raincoat over his arm, he approached the barrier with the confidence of one who hasn't a care in the world.

Marcel allowed him to pass through, surrendering his ticket, and then touched him on the arm. 'Excuse me, monsieur, but may I see your passport?' he asked politely.

The man's expression changed. The confidence gave way to an anxiety he was unable to conceal. 'Why do you want my passport?' he asked, shortly.

'A matter of formality, monsieur. We are police officers and we are looking for someone.'

The man – they still did not know his name – produced a blue and gold British passport from his pocket.

Marcel took it, turned to the photograph on the first page and compared it with the face watching him.

'You are Monsieur George Bardello?' said he.

'Yes.'

Marcel went through the visa pages. 'When did you enter France, monsieur?'

'Er – yesterday.'

'How is it that your passport carries no stamp of entry?'

The man must have realized then that he was trapped. The colour fled from his cheeks, leaving them ashen. 'No one – no one has asked me for my passport,' he stammered, although he must have known that he could not hope to get away with such a flimsy excuse.

'I wonder how that could have happened,' said Marcel, blandly. 'May I see what you have in your portfolio?'

That did it. For a second or two Bardello, his lips compressed, stared at Marcel as if trying to read from his expression how much he really knew. Apparently he decided, from the attitudes of the three men confronting him, that he was trapped, and made a desperate bid to escape, hurling himself at his accusers. He broke through them, too, but only to find himself in the grip of the gendarmes, who acted with a speed which showed they had been ready for just such a move. Then, as if realizing that his case was hopeless, he allowed himself without a struggle to be led to the waiting police car.

Marcel picked up the portfolio, which had been dropped, and opened it. Without a word he showed the contents to the others. It was stuffed with bundles of English one-pound notes.

Biggles nodded. 'I thought it might be something like that,' he said quietly. 'We shall soon know all about it. He'll talk when he sees he's beaten. I know the type. I'll leave you to take care of him until we can get home and send over extradition papers. In a simple case like this it shouldn't take long.'

Biggles was right when he said he thought Bardello

would talk. Caught with the proceeds of a mail-bag robbery on him and with his fingerprints on the joystick of the crashed Tiger Moth, he broke down under questioning and confessed.

An ex-air gunner of the R.A.F., in which he had served with Crayford, he had on his discharge drifted into crime to become a member of a London gang of car bandits. These he had double-crossed, bolting with the proceeds of a mail-van robbery. Aware that their revenge would be swift if they caught him, his problem then had been to get out of England. He had gone to Holmwood, purely by chance, in the hope of stealing an aircraft. There he had seen, and renewed acquaintance with, Crayford. It was then that this plan had been conceived. He had asked Crayford to give him a 'flip' for old times' sake. Crayford had pointed out that he was not yet qualified to carry passengers; but, foolishly, and fatally as it transpired, he had allowed himself to be persuaded into a breach of regulations by picking up his passenger in a near-by field.

As soon as they were in the air Bardello had struck his pilot on the head with his revolver, which left him in possession of the aircraft, with what result we know. All that remained was to fake the crash, a scheme that might well have succeeded had it not been for the swift action and co-operation of the Air Police.

Bardello declared that he had no intention of killing Crayford; his intention had been merely to stun him. But this, from a man with a criminal record, cut no ice with a hard-headed jury, and in due course the man who was both thief and murderer paid the usual penalty.

10

THE MAN WHO
CAME BY NIGHT

IT was a phone call from Inspector Gaskin, of Scotland
Yard, that took Air Detective-Inspector Bigglesworth
and his police pilot Ginger Hebblethwaite to the North
Hampshire village of Shotsey. They met the Inspector,
with the local police sergeant at the churchyard gate.

'I thought you'd better have a look at this,' the
bowler-hatted Inspector told Biggles. 'It looks to be up
your street.' He led the way to a small isolated building.

'What's this place?' asked Biggles.

'Mortuary.'

'Nothing nasty, I hope?'

'It might have been worse,' stated the Inspector, as
the sergeant unlocked the door. They went in.

On the bench lay the body of a slim, good-looking
lad of not more than seventeen or eighteen. On a side-
table lay the clothes he had presumably been wearing
when he had met his death. Conspicuous were a flying
jacket, cap and goggles. Water dripping from them had
formed a puddle. On the floor lay a mass of wet rag
that was clearly an unfurled parachute.

'Where did you find this?' asked Biggles.

'In the lake, in the park opposite,' answered the Inspector. 'Property of Colonel Linder. His hobby's fishing. Once every so often the lake's drained to clean out the pike that eat the trout. The gamekeeper did the draining, which simply meant opening a floodgate at the lower end. This lay on the mud. He fetched the police sergeant. The county police called me. Seeing it was a flying job I called you.'

'Have you identified him?'

'No. He isn't British. At least, no one's missing in this country. The only thing he had on him was this. It was in a ticket pocket. Might have been a lucky charm or something.' The Inspector showed a French fifty-franc piece through which a hole had been punched. 'He must have deliberately removed all marks of identification.'

'Which means he knew he was taking a chance on something.'

'He knew all right.' The Inspector picked up a haversack, obviously heavy. 'This is what he had on him – probably helped to drown him. Nice little lot of expensive Swiss watches. Must be two or three hundred.'

'So we know what he was doing,' said Biggles slowly, taking a cigarette from his case. 'Poor little beggar. He's only a kid. I wonder what skunk got him into the smuggling racket. How long has he been dead?'

'The doctor says three days. Death due to drowning.'

Biggles nodded. 'The picture's pretty plain. He wasn't alone in the racket. Someone dropped him from a plane – in the wrong place. He fell in the drink and couldn't get out. His job was to hand the watches to a confederate, after which he would have been picked up somewhere and flown home.'

'He could have made his own way home if a pal had given him a ticket and some money.'

'For that he would have needed a passport, in which case it would have been in his pocket. How many people know about this?'

'The squire, the keeper, the doctor and us.'

'Good. Try to keep it out of the newspapers for a few days. The inquest can be postponed pending inquiries. That will keep the pilot of the plane guessing and give me a chance to find him. That shouldn't be too difficult. For obvious reasons the machine that unloaded this poor fellow into a death trap must have been privately owned – and flown. Air line pilots don't play this sort of game. The drop would hardly be made in broad daylight for all the world to see so we can judge the time. Mind if I use your phone, sergeant?'

'This way, sir.'

As they walked to the police station the Inspector remarked: 'That coin suggests the boy came from France.'

'Not only the coin. The parachute is a French type. The boy looks French, anyway.'

From the station Biggles put a call through to his operations room. Algy Lacey answered. Said Biggles: 'Get me out a detailed met. report for last Sunday night. Wind velocity southern region is important. Tell Bertie to check all airports for continental, particularly French, privately-owned aircraft, landing during the hours of darkness on the same night. You might also check with radar for unidentified aircraft. That's all. I'm on my way home.'

When Biggles and Ginger arrived at headquarters two hours later Algy and Bertie had completed their respective tasks.

Algy reported that the weather on the night in question had been clear and fine, with the moon in the first quarter. At midnight, from dead calm, a wind of 30 m.p.h. had sprung up from the south-east.

Algy was able to state that radar had a nil report. There was a record of only one private aircraft landing at an authorized Customs airport. A French Cigale light plane, F-XXZL, had landed at Gatwick shortly after midnight. The pilot was flying solo. He was well known there as a French businessman who dealt in antique clocks and watches. His name was Monsieur Claude Vauvine. His documents were in order. He had cleared Customs, spent the night in London, where he had a branch shop in Mayfair, and had returned to France the following day.

'Something tells me he had other business interests over here,' murmured Biggles, and went on to explain to Algy and Bertie the purpose of the inquiries. 'I'd say it was the wind that did the mischief,' he surmised. 'The pilot would no doubt get a weather report when he started. The wind got up after he was in the air with the result that his accomplice fell in the lake. Had he known there was a thirty mile an hour wind he wouldn't have risked the jump at all – unless he was a fool.'

Biggles made a mark on the large-scale map of the

district. 'It must have been about here that the boy with the watches intended to touch down. Algy, take the Auster and check up on the open ground in that area. You might take a strip of photos while you're at it. Bertie, go and have a look at what Monsieur Vauvine sells at his shop in Mayfair. I'm going to slip over to France for a word with Marcel Brissac. Ginger, you might ring Marcel at the Sûreté and ask him to meet us. I shall land at Le Bourget. Say I want particulars of Mr Claude Vauvine who owns a Cigale, registration F-XXZL.'

It was three o'clock when Biggles and Ginger, in the police Proctor, landed at the Paris airport of Le Bourget to find Marcel Brissac, their French opposite number, waiting.

'What do we have cooking this time, Beegles, old dog?' inquired Marcel.

'Did you put the spotlight on Monsieur Vauvine?'

'But of course. Is he a naughty boy?'

'He might be.'

'He is a member of the Flying Club of Tornay, where he has his own machine, a Cigale, F-XXZL. It is, he says, useful in his business, which makes much travelling, for he has several shops in Europe. You know he went to England late on Sunday.'

'Yes. Where did he clear Customs over this side?'

'Here, at Le Bourget. He was alone. He took with him some of those old French clocks that have dancing figures on the face. Tell me, old cabbage, does this have a nasty smell – *hein*?'

'I detect a slight aroma.' Biggles explained the case, briefly. 'If Vauvine is our man he must have picked up his assistant after he had checked out, probably between here and the coast, possibly at Tornay, which is in the right direction. Do you mind if we run down and make a few discreet inquiries? This is your affair as well as mine. Someone brought those watches into France from Switzerland.'

'Let us go,' agreed Marcel. 'Louis Boulenger, the manager, who is also the chief instructor, is a friend of mine.'

They all got into the Proctor, which in twenty minutes was standing on the tarmac of the flying club. A middle-aged, jovial-looking man came over to them. Marcel introduced Boulenger, who cleared the air a lot by his own first question. 'The police have come, no doubt, to find my missing mechanic, Lucien Mallon,' he remarked shrewdly.

'When did you last see him?' asked Marcel.

'On Sunday afternoon.'

Biggles stepped in. 'Did he by any chance go off with Monsieur Vauvine on Sunday night?'

'But no,' answered the instructor, looking surprised. 'Monsieur Vauvine went off alone, about seven o'clock. Later he came back, saying he had forgotten something.'

'It would be dark then.'

'Yes, it was dark; but Monsieur Vauvine is an old war pilot and often flies by night.'

'He was still alone when he took off the second time?'

'He does not say he is taking anyone. It is dark so I do not see.' The instructor looked from one to the other. 'You think he could have taken Lucien? If he did he did not bring him back, for I saw him return alone on Monday.'

Biggles went on. 'This Lucien Mallon. Would he be about seventeen, with black hair, a spot under his left eye and a little scar on his chin?'

'That is Lucien,' declared the instructor. 'I am worried. What shall I tell his mother if I have lost him, after I persuade her to let him come to me as apprentice?'

'Sooner or later you will have to tell her the truth, my friend,' said Biggles sadly. 'In strict confidence, he is dead.'

Boulenger stared incredulously. 'But that is not possible,' he cried.

'He jumped by parachute over England but fell in a lake and was drowned,' said Marcel. 'Now you know why we are here.'

'But Monsieur Vauvine did not tell me! Why?'

'He had a reason,' returned Marcel grimly. 'Presently I will tell you what it was. For the moment, not a word of this to anyone, or we may never catch the man who was responsible for Lucien's death. I must ask you to do this. The next time Monsieur Vauvine fills his tanks for a business trip will you please phone me at the Sûreté?'

'Certainly.'

'*Bon*. That is all for now. Remember, silence. I'll tell you the rest of the story later. *Au revoir*.'

'*Au revoir, monsieur*.'

Biggles dropped Marcel at Le Bourget and went on to England, to find the set of air photographs, taken by Algy, on his desk.

They revealed what might have been expected; several large fields, adjacent, without hedges, trees or buildings of any sort; in a word, an ideal place for a parachute landing. The fact that it occurred where the dead smuggler would have touched down had there been no wind, could not, Biggles asserted, be coincidence. The area was bounded by a single second-class road. The nearest railway-station was five miles away.

'As our nocturnal visitor would hardly be likely to walk five miles with a load of contraband it's safe to assume that someone was waiting on that road with a car,' surmised Biggles. 'We shall be there too, next time, I hope.'

Bertie's report on the Mayfair establishment of Monsieur Vauvine was equally significant. It was a double-fronted shop. One side was devoted to antiques, but the other window exposed for sale a selection of expensive new watches.

'All we can do now,' said Biggles, 'is to wait till we hear from Marcel.'

It was a fortnight before the expected phone call came through. Apart from reporting that Vauvine was at Le Bourget, clearing customs for a flight to London, Marcel had another interesting piece of news. Two days earlier, Vauvine, who was under police surveillance, had gone by road to Pontade, on the Swiss frontier, where he had spent the night. After dark he had gone for a walk. While he was out, an aircraft, flying low, had passed over. It had come from the direction of the frontier and had returned that way. Marcel was convinced that while it was over France it had made a 'droppage' of contraband, but rather than risk making a mistake he had left things to take their course in the hope that Biggles would catch the smuggler red-handed.

In ten minutes the police car was on its way to the suspected Hampshire dropping ground.

It was a fine night, clear and still, when it arrived and cruised down the boundary road, watch being kept on both sides. Half-way down Ginger spotted what he was looking for. The headlamps of their own car shone for a moment on the metal fittings of a stationary car, showing no lights, that had been backed into the grass entrance of a field.

'There he is,' murmured Ginger.

Biggles did not alter speed until he had rounded the next bend, when he switched off his lights, turned, pulled into the side of the road and cut the engine.

'You all know the drill,' he said, getting out. 'I'll take Ginger with me and get as near the car as is possible without being seen. Bertie, when you hear the machine, get up on the hedge and try to see where the parachute lands. You'll know the moment the drop has been made because the machine will almost certainly turn away. Algy, you stay at the wheel ready to move fast. Should the car up the road try to bolt turn across the road and block it.'

'I get it.'

'Come on, Ginger.' Keeping on the grass verge Biggles began a cautious approach to the unknown car. There was no other traffic.

The time could not have been better judged, for within ten minutes, by which time they were close to the car, the distant hum of a light plane told them that the new-type smuggler was on his way. Ginger's eyes probed the starry heavens for navigation lights but could see none. The aircraft came on.

The watchers on the ground were still creeping

forward when the aero engine died for perhaps ten seconds, and then, coming on again, began to recede.

Ginger's pulses beat faster, for he realized that somewhere in the darkness overhead a parachute was on its way to the ground. Biggles climbed up the bank and looked over the hedge. He was down in a moment, whispering: 'Here he comes.'

At that instant the engine of the waiting car was switched on, as were the lights, obviously to reveal its position. Biggles, with Ginger at his heels, moved swiftly towards it, but froze as the door was opened and a man stepped out. A few seconds later the night raider, a haversack on his shoulder, carrying his parachute in a loose bundle, ran up, breathing heavily from excitement or exertion – perhaps both.

The driver of the car was taking the haversack when Biggles stepped in. 'I'm a police officer –' he began, and then had to break off, ducking, as the man swung the heavy bag at his head.

Dodging the blow, he jumped forward to grab his man, now sliding back into his seat, only to have the car door slammed in his face. The gears clashed and the car shot forward, but not before Biggles had mounted the running board. His whistle shrilled.

The parachutist, a youth like his even more unlucky predecessor, made no effort to get away. Encumbered as he was with heavy clothing it would have been futile, anyway. He seemed stunned with shock, and did not resist when Ginger put on the handcuffs.

As Ginger took his prisoner down the road he could

see the two cars together, the police car broadside on. By the time he had reached them the driver of the other car, with his road blocked and three officers to deal with, had submitted to arrest.

After the cars had been moved to clear the road Biggles took the parachutist, who still seemed dazed by the speed of events, to one side, and spoke to him quietly in French. 'Do you know what was in that bag you carried?'

'*Non, monsieur.*' The answer was given so frankly that Ginger felt sure the lad was not lying.

'Why did you do it?' asked Biggles.

'For adventure, monsieur.' Ginger smiled at this naïve reply.

'What were you to do with the bag?'

'I was to give it to the monsieur who would be waiting with the car.'

'And then?'

'He would take me to Monsieur Vauvine who would fly me back to France.'

Biggles turned to Ginger. 'Send a signal to the chief,' he ordered. 'Tell him the birds are in the bag. Vauvine can be picked up at Gatwick. The parachutist has named him as the man who flew him over. We're on our way home.'

So ended another smuggling scheme that may have looked safe to the man who organized it, but reckoned without the Air Police. He, and the driver of the car, who turned out to be the manager of the shop in Mayfair, are now serving long prison sentences, apart from losing some hundreds of valuable watches and paying triple duty on them.

The parachutist, whose desire for adventure may have blinded him to the seriousness of what he was doing, his age and a clean record being taken into account, was soon back in France, a badly shaken, and, it is to be hoped, wiser young man.

11

THE BIRD THAT
DIED OF DIAMONDS

'IF,' said Air Commodore Raymond, of the Special Air Police, 'if only crooks would turn their fertile imaginations to legal operations they would fare far better than they do by crime.'

Biggles' eyes went to three diamonds that sparkled on his chief's desk. 'Very nice, too,' he remarked, smiling. 'Where did you find those?'

'I won't waste time by asking you to guess because you never would,' returned the Air Commodore. 'The large one came from the breast of a pheasant. Of the smaller ones, one came from its wing and the other from its leg.'

'Are you talking about a live pheasant?'

'It was alive until it got in the way of these stones.'

'The bird didn't have a string of pearls round its neck by any chance?' bantered Biggles.

'No. But it might have done.' The Air Commodore pushed the cigarette box forward. 'Sit down and I'll tell you a tale that would have made Hans Anderson blush.'

Biggles lit a cigarette. 'Go ahead, sir; I'm listening.'

Raymond proceeded. 'There lives, in Scotland, where he has an estate called Tomlecht, a retired Army Colonel named Colin McGill. He's a friend of mine. Like many landowners, to meet taxation he's been forced to take paying guests for the shooting season. He gets them by advertising in high-class sporting papers. In the spring he received a reply to such an advertisement from a Baron Zorrall who at the time of writing was at Monte Carlo for the pigeon shooting competitions. To make a longish story short it was arranged that the Baron should arrive at Tomlecht on October 15 for the pheasant shooting. In due course his guns arrived, in one of those cases which has a cartridge magazine attached. The Baron, however, did not arrive, either on the date fixed or later. There was not a word from him; wherefore after a time the Colonel wrote to him at the Monte Carlo address, an hotel, asking him what he wanted him to do with the guns.'

'To which the hotel replied saying the Baron wasn't there.'

The Air Commodore frowned. 'Don't spoil my story by anticipating. The hotel said more than that. No person by the name of Baron Zorrall had ever stayed there. The Colonel promptly opened the gun case to make sure it contained guns. It did, and two boxes of cartridges, one of No. 7 shot and the other of No. 4. The guns and cartridges, incidentally, were of French make.' The Air Commodore stubbed his cigarette.

'Now towards the end of the season,' he resumed, 'the Colonel wanted a pheasant for the table, but finding he had run out of number four cartridges he borrowed a few from the Baron's box. With one of these he shot a pheasant which in due course appeared on the dinner-table. To bite on a lead pellet in a game bird is not an uncommon occurrence, as you may have discovered; but to bite on a diamond must be a rare experience. If the Colonel is to be believed it's also an uncomfortable one. One can imagine his astonishment when, removing the offending object from his mouth, he discovered what it was. Carefully dissecting the carcass of this remarkable bird he found two more diamonds – but no lead shot; from which he was forced to the incredible conclusion that he had killed his dinner with a charge of gems. That the cartridge had been loaded with them was beyond doubt.'

Biggles grinned. 'Delicious. This beats the goose that laid the golden eggs.'

'The Colonel did the obvious thing,' went on the Air Commodore. 'He cut open another cartridge. It was loaded with rubies. Others contained matching pearls, obviously a broken-down necklace. In a word, while the number seven cartridges were loaded with lead shot the number fours were loaded with precious stones. He made another discovery. In the box of number sevens, which apparently had never been opened, he found an advice note from the French suppliers, addressed to a Prince Boris Devronik, presumably an *alias* of Baron Zorrall, for, among other things, a box of empty cases which presumably he intended to load himself.'

'With sparklers.'

'Of course. The Colonel rang me up and at my request sent the whole works to me. So far the story has been fact. We must now introduce a little surmise. We may suppose that the problem of this phoney

Baron, or Prince, was to get certain stones, probably stolen, into this country without declaring them to the Customs people. He hit on the bright idea of loading cartridges with them, and sending them, with his guns, as registered luggage to Scotland. He got away with it, too, for as we know, they arrived. He followed, breaking his journey in London, where he took a room at the Crestata Hotel.'

'You know that?'

'Yes. I'll tell you how we know, presently. That he did not go on to Scotland was due to the fact that during the night, in his room, someone slipped a stiletto into his heart. The Yard could find no motive for the crime and the murderer was never caught.'

Biggles nodded. 'I remember the case.'

'What we knew, but did not reveal to the Press while we were looking for the murderer, was that the dead man's name was Zorrall, an international jewel thief. We suspected he had been stabbed by an accomplice whom he had double-crossed. The only clue we had to the murderer was fingerprints; there were plenty of those but they were unknown to us. They were small enough to have been made by a woman. This, and the fact that there were fingerprints at all, suggests an amateur did the job. Apart from us having no record a professional crook would have been more careful.'

'What about the stones?' asked Biggles. 'Have they been traced?'

'Yes. These stones on the table were part of the fruits of a robbery at the Villa of the Countess Castelano, on the Riviera, in the South of France. Zorrall must have done the job. Having prised the gems from their settings he hid them in the cartridges, got them out of the country as has now been revealed and followed on himself. Had he not been murdered he would have collected the stuff in Scotland and that would have been that. Someone in the know followed him, killed him, and ransacked his luggage for the jewels, without, of course, finding them.'

'Was anyone suspected of the robbery at the time?'

'The Countess's maid, an elderly widow, was suspected of being concerned with it. But she didn't do the killing because on the night in question she was certainly in France, and the fingerprints were not hers. So the story ties up pretty well – except that we haven't got the murderer. Any ideas?'

'Did Zorrall actually take part in the pigeon shooting at Monte Carlo?'

'Yes. He's a first-class shot.'

'Then the accomplice, presumably the murderer, would know he had a pair of guns. Obviously he didn't know where they'd gone, or not finding the jewels in London would have guessed they were in the gun case and followed the guns to Scotland. He must have wondered where those guns went, and as the recovery of the jewels has never been announced he will assume the stones are still with them. It's likely that he's still looking for them. Any mention of a pair of guns belonging to Baron Zorrall, therefore, should prove an irresistible bait to the murderer.'

'How would you bring the guns to his notice?'

'The most likely place for guns to be mentioned would be in the best sporting journals. There's a chance that the murderer may watch such magazines. Our only chance of catching him now would be

through those guns; and if he knew that Zorrall sometimes went to Scotland for the shooting it should
narrow the field considerably.'

'I follow your argument,' said the Air Commodore.
'What exactly would you do?'

'I'd run an advertisement in the English and French
sporting magazines, particularly those read in the
South of France, to the effect that Baron Zorrall is requested to collect his guns from Colonel McGill, Tomlecht, Morayshire, Scotland, otherwise they will be sold
to defray expenses. If the man who killed Zorrall sees
that he'll apply for the guns, or come in person to
collect them.'

'That's assuming he has the money to pay for them.
A pair of high-class guns are today worth from three
to five hundred pounds.'

'If he's a professional crook, as we suppose,
not having the money shouldn't stop him. Knowing
what the jewels are worth he'd take any risk to get
them.'

'Your plan means sending the guns back to Scotland.'

'Of course.' Biggles smiled. 'It wouldn't be much
use inviting a murderer to come *here* for them. I'll
take them to Scotland myself if you like, and hang
around for a bit to see if anyone shows up. A spot of
Highland air wouldn't do me any harm. You might
have a word with Colonel McGill and put him wise as
to what's cooking.'

'All right,' agreed the Air Commodore. 'It is, as you
say, our only chance. If the scheme doesn't come off
it will have done no harm.'

In planning to trap the murderer of Zorrall, jewel thief and smuggler, Biggles did not expect him to arrive immediately at Colonel McGill's house in Scotland. He thought it far more likely that the man would make a written application for the guns, at all events in the first place, to confirm that they were really the ones he sought. What he would do then was an open question, and would probably depend on the man's financial position. He would hardly expect the Colonel to send him the guns without either the money or some proof of his claim to them. If he could produce neither money nor proof, then he would, Biggles was confident, employ other means to get them. If, as was suspected, the man was a professional thief, this would not be difficult.

It need hardly be said that to guard against accident the cartridges in which the gems had been hidden had been replaced by ordinary lead shot.

Colonel McGill, who was now a party to the scheme, undertook to show Biggles any letters that came in answer to the advertisement about the guns. Biggles was sure – too sure, as it transpired – that such a letter would come; and for this reason, although he was staying with the Colonel, he was nearly taken by surprise when things did not pan out as he expected.

The gun case, smothered with international hotel labels, was put on the cleaning bench in the gun-room, with game bags, cartridge boxes and the usual paraphernalia of such places. The gun-room, as is so often the case, was not actually in the house, but formed part of a separate building in the courtyard, just outside the back door.

Rather than upset the household Biggles had elected to sleep in an unused ghillie's bothy that was an extension of the gun-room. There was no connecting door. That is to say, in order to get from the bothy to the gun-room it would be necessary to go outside and enter it by its own door. Both rooms were fitted with electric light.

Ten days passed without incident. No letter arrived. No visitor called, and Biggles was beginning to feel he was wasting his time when the trap was sprung in a manner that he had not foreseen.

He had gone to bed as usual just before midnight after spending the evening with his host, talking mostly about shooting. Also, as usual, he was soon asleep.

Some time later he awoke with the sudden start that is caused by a strange sound penetrating the unconscious mind. He was wide awake on the instant. What had caused the sound he did not know. All he knew was, something had awakened him, and as is usual in such circumstances he lay perfectly still in the darkness, listening intently. The silence was profound. A square of dim moonlight showed the position of the window.

At last there came what he was waiting for: a repetition of the sound. It was very slight, but hard, as of metal on metal. It came, without doubt, from the room next door – the gun-room. He thought it might be a gamekeeper preparing for a night patrol but he decided to make sure.

Getting up and slipping a dressing-gown over his pyjamas he moved silently to the door of the bothy and looked out. He could see no one. No light came from the gun-room window, which was of course significant, for an authorized person would certainly switch on the light. A few steps took him to the gun-room window. He looked in. Against the glow of an electric torch, near the bench, a figure was moving. On the bench lay the gun case, conspicuous by its many labels. It was open.

With infinite care Biggles moved on to the door. It was ajar. His hand felt for the electric light switch. At the click the room was flooded with light.

The person at the bench spun round with a gasp of alarm, and Biggles saw, to his astonishment, that it was a youth of about sixteen. He wore a black beret. He looked terrified.

'Who are you and what are you doing here?' demanded Biggles sternly, for he knew the boy was not one of the staff. If he was slow in grasping the truth it was probably because he could not associate this frightened-looking youth with the sort of man he expected.

'M . . . monsieur,' stammered the boy.

'Are you alone?' rapped out Biggles, glancing around.

'Oui, monsieur.'

Biggles pointed to the gun case. 'What are you doing with that?'

The boy had difficulty in speaking.

'Is that what you came here for – from France,' went on Biggles.

'Oui, monsieur.' The words were hardly audible.

Now this was not the sort of situation Biggles had anticipated, and he looked at the boy critically. 'You don't look like a thief,' he opined.

'I am not a thief, *monsieur*.'

'Then what are you looking for? Could it be some – stolen property?'

The boy made a gesture of resignation. 'I see you know,' he said simply. 'I have done my best and failed. You must do as you wish with me.'

Biggles pointed to a chair. 'Sit down and tell me all you know of this – the truth.'

There, in the gun-room, the boy told his story.

For twenty years his mother, a widow, had worked for the Contessa Castelàno. He, Pierre Pastor, a schoolboy at the time of the robbery, also lived in the villa. Everyone was happy until a man named Baron Zorrall had arrived on the scene. The Baron had taken his mother out and later asked her to marry him, to which, being in love with him, she agreed. He, Pierre, had never trusted the man, for, as he averred, why should this rich man want to marry an old woman? Suspicious, he had watched Zorrall, and when one day he had seen him take his guns to the station he knew he was going away, for they were addressed to a place in Scotland. The next day he saw the Baron's luggage go, addressed to the Crestata Hotel, London; but he said nothing to his mother for fear of upsetting her.

That afternoon the Contessa went to a party. Pierre's mother had gone out to meet Zorrall by an appointment which he did not keep. The villa was empty. Zorrall knew that, and it was then the jewels were stolen. Pierre had no doubt as to who had taken them. Knowing where his mother kept her money he had taken it and followed Zorrall to London to make him give up the jewels.

'Why didn't you go to the police?' asked Biggles.

'I was a fool. But my mother was in love with this villain and I hoped to avoid a scandal.'

'How did you get into England at that time without a passport?'

'I said my mother was in front. I had lost her. Seeing I was only a boy they let me through the barrier. I went to Zorrall's room at the hotel, and found him there, opening letters with a knife. I asked for the jewels, saying if he did not give them to me I would tell the police. He hit me on the face many times. Then he took me by the neck and shook me. What could I do? He was a big man. I snatched up the knife and struck back at him. He fell on the floor. Swiftly I search his luggage. The jewels are not there. Then I know they have gone to Scotland with the guns, and as I cannot remember the address I must go home without them. To my mother I said nothing. She was ill with grief. She thought Zorrall had taken her money with the jewels.'

'Did you know that Zorrall died from your blow?'

Pierre's eyes opened wide, horror dawning in them. 'I did not know, *monsieur*, for I did not see the newspapers.'

'Where is your mother now?'

'She still works for the Contessa. So do I, saving my money to repay her. Always I read the papers to see if the jewels are found. They are not. But I see a notice about the guns. I remember the address, then, for it was the same that Zorrall had put on his guns when he went to London. I ask for a passport for a holiday in England for now I am old enough to have one. I come here. Now you know why, *monsieur*. What must I do?'

'Tomorrow you will come with me to London,' answered Biggles. 'Later, the Contessa will have her jewels.'

At Pierre's trial, all the circumstances being known, it was held that he struck Zorrall in self-defence and was discharged.

These are other Knight Books

Henry Treece

HOUNDS OF THE KING

1066 – the field of what is now called Hastings. The Hounds of the King, Harold's personal warriors, gather for the last time to protect their king against the Normans.

One of these warriors is Beornoth, and this book is about his life in Harold's service. It is a story of heroism and adventure, and a magnificent picture of Saxon England.

Geoffrey Trease

THE HILLS OF VARNA

The year is 1609. A University brawl sends Alan Drayton fugitive across Europe seeking an ancient manuscript.

In Venice, at the house of Aldus Manutius, the famous printer, he meets Angela. From then on she shares his adventures: Adriatic piracy, blood feuds, wild Turkish riders, the sinister Monks of Varna. And always, in the shadows, stalks their arch-enemy and rival, Cesare Morelli, crafty, clever and unscrupulous.

Acknowledged by many critics to be the best and most exciting of all historical adventure stories by this renowned novelist.

Willard Price

SOUTH SEA ADVENTURE

Commissioned to bring back a collection of dangerous sea creatures, Hal and Roger Hunt sail for the little-known islands of the west Pacific in a chartered schooner. They have an additional errand: to visit and examine the pearl-oyster beds of a secret lagoon, and it is this which brings them into the greatest danger – greater even than capturing a huge sea bat, or weathering a hurricane.

Falcon Travis

FIRST KNIGHT BOOK OF PUZZLES

This new book has everything for the puzzle enthusiast – word, picture and number puzzles, general knowledge quizzes, crosswords with a difference, secret codes, and lots of new puzzles which you won't have come across before.

These are other Knight Books

Michael Deakin

TOM GRATTAN'S WAR

Three stories of adventure and suspense, set in Yorkshire at the time of the First World War and based on the television series. Tom Grattan finds himself with spies – he sees a most curious war machine – he helps repair a crashed plane against time – he has to show true heroism in saving the lives of some prisoners-of-war.

Paul Berna

THRESHOLD OF THE STARS

Young Michael Jousse's account of a momentous year on a research station in France, during which plans are made for a landing on the moon. It is a story of hopes and fears, success and disaster, with all the time sinister signs of sabotage and spies.

These are other Knight Books

Falcon Travis

CAMPING AND HIKING

This is a new book – written, designed and illustrated to be a guide for anyone who is going camping or hiking, whether alone, with a few friends, or in a larger party.
From equipment and personal gear to striking camp and packing up at the end, there is something of interest to everyone, however experienced they are. The extra material covers many vital and fascinating aspects of life in the country – maps and compasses, knives and axes, first aid, logs and nature diaries, weather and safety precautions. The book is published with the support and approval of the Scout Association, and covers almost all the tests for the Scout Standard and Advanced Scout Standard.

Ask your local bookseller, or at your public library, for details of other Knight Books, or write to the Editor-in-Chief, Knight Books, Arlen House, Salisbury Road, Leicester LE1 7QS